Nell
of Blue
Harbor

Nell of Blue Harbor

MARION DOREN

Harcourt Brace Jovanovich, Publishers

SAN DIEGO   NEW YORK   LONDON

Requests for permission to make copies of any part of the work should be
mailed to: Permissions Department, Harcourt Brace Jovanovich, Publishers,
Orlando, Florida 32887.

Library of Congress Cataloging-in-Publication Data
Doren, Marion Walker.
Nell of Blue Harbor/by Marion Doren.
p. cm.
Summary: Eleven-year-old Nell is forced to grow up quickly when she moves
from a Vermont commune to the real world with parents not yet ready to
accept their responsibilities.
ISBN 0-15-256889-1
[1. Parent and child—Fiction.   2. Communal living—Fiction.]
I. Title.
PZ7.D7274Ne   1990
[Fic]—dc20   89-24505

Printed in the United States of America

First edition

A B C D E

For my children:
Anne, Martin, Keith, and Laurie

1

The March sun rose behind bare branches as Nell Willow tiptoed out of the cabin. Her parents, Tip and Ilse, and baby sister, Abigail, still slept, but early morning was Nell's time to visit the lambs.

"Hi, babies," she crooned by the wire fence. The lambs leaped sideways, landing on stiff legs, tiny hooves cutting into Vermont's frozen earth. She called to her favorite, a little black-faced lamb. "Here, Blackie," she said softly as she slowly reached through the fence.

"Don't grow up," Nell warned him. "You'll get fat like your mother." The ewes plodded heavily around the rocky field, rooting up bits of last year's grass while their babies nuzzled them. Nell found it hard to believe that sprightly little Blackie would change into a heavy animal wearing tangled, dirty wool instead of his soft curls.

The bell outside the dining hall clanged its loud wake-up order, calling Nell back to begin a new day. Tip said a bugle had roused him when he was in the army, and Ilse had wakened to an alarm clock at college. Nell had known only the sound of the bronze bell in the eleven years of her life.

She watched Blackie charge at the other lambs, butting their heads and bleating high *ma-a-a*s. Her dream was to have a pet all her own, but pets were against The Farm's rules. "Animals are here to feed and clothe us, not just to be played with," one of the adults had told her. Reluctantly, she turned back toward the cabin, leaving the quiet morning behind her.

The second bell called every member of The Farm to breakfast. Tip and Ilse would not worry that Nell had already left the cabin. She never missed a meal, never went outside the fence that circled The Farm, and never broke the rules. She had lived on The Farm since she was born, and she loved every inch and every minute of it.

Nell saw her family up ahead on the frozen path. Tip and Ilse walked shoulder to shoulder as Ilse pushed Abigail's stroller, giving the baby a bumpy ride that made her laugh with delight. Nell was content to walk behind and consider what a nice-looking couple her parents were, in spite of Tip's limp. Ilse looked as if she belonged somewhere else instead of on The Farm, and sometimes a hint of sadness touched her face when she talked of college days. But she played the part of a farm woman, and no one could complain about her gardens or the woolen things she wove.

Tip and Ilse were different from the rest of the people on The Farm, Nell thought as she followed behind. Ilse drifted through the days, spinning and weaving, or gardening in the warm weather. Tip was given easy jobs because of the shrapnel in his head and the brace on his leg. An exploding grenade had nearly killed him in Vietnam. He fed the animals or wrote feed orders, but he did not dig the stumps or the boulders that kept pushing their way into the fields. The other adults on The Farm ran the tractor and sheared the sheep, made some of the clothes, and cooked the food. They were the workers.

After the war, Tip and some other veterans had pooled their money and established The Farm—a place where they could plant things, raise animals, and make their living from the land. They turned their backs on politics and pollution and worked together to create a better place for themselves and their families.

Ilse had not been excused from the heavier work. She simply did not know how to cook or clean, and the women found it easier to do the work themselves than to try to teach her.

Tip, Ilse, and Abigail entered the dining hall ahead of Nell. It had once been a cow barn, but now it was a place for people; its cool, dusty air filled with the aroma of coffee. When Nell grew up she wanted to work in the kitchen in the early morning and be the first to smell the coffee perking and the bread baking.

Nell shrugged off her jacket and slipped onto the bench next to Abigail's baby seat.

Tip smiled. "Have a good visit?" he asked.

She touched his curled right hand. "Blackie came right up to me and let me pet him." She felt her face warm up. "He kind of reminds me of you."

Tip's hand pressed her fingers lightly.

Without looking up, Ilse said, "This year I'm going

to plant the herbs in a knot pattern. It's an old patchwork quilt design." She traced a knot on the wooden table with her long, tapered finger. Ilse looked elegant even in blue jeans and a work shirt, her long blond hair tied back with a bandanna.

"I don't see what you're making such a fuss about," Tip said softly. The war had taken part of his voice away. "Parsley is still parsley no matter what design you plant it in."

"It may taste the same," Ilse said, "but I'll feel better when I see it laid out in the pattern. Even words in a poem look better when they're laid out right." Ilse wanted everything to be perfect.

Nell smoothed her dark curls, ruffled by the March wind, then guided Abigail's juice cup to the baby's mouth before she could tip it over. Being perfect was hard, but Nell was determined to be perfect like her mother.

Tip stood up first when breakfast was over. "Come on, baby." He lifted year-old Abigail and slid her into her stroller. She rode happily to the pillowed corner where the Wee Ones gathered. Today, Alice Jones was the caretaker, and she was taking them to see the lambs.

Nell watched Alice stuff four babies into snowsuits, put large pillows into a cart, and arrange the children among the pillows. Four babies in one year was a lot. The Farm was growing.

Ilse pulled on her work gloves. "Learn lots for me," she said. Nell wrinkled her nose. Just last night her mother had talked again about her college days and how happy she'd been when she was studying. Nell already knew how to read. If she was going to work in the kitchen when she was older, she didn't need much more learning.

"Why don't *you* teach us?" Nell asked.

Ilse smoothed her gloved fingers. "I don't think I'm patient enough to stand four hours with children. I was trained to teach college students, who know how to sit quietly and listen." She clapped her hands together and headed for the door. Nell knew her mother's mind was on her plans for the garden layout. When Ilse fixed her attention on something, she didn't hear or see anything else.

Nell sat at the end of the cleared table reserved for the Big Ones. There were three of them. Nell was the first child born after The Farm had been established, and she had just turned eleven a month ago. Bobby Moore and Chrissie Grady were both ten.

Eight Middle Ones, from five to nine, sat at the other end of the table. The two- to four-year-olds had no name, though Nell thought of them as the In-betweenies. There were ten of them in another corner of the room.

"I wonder who's teaching us this week," Nell said to Chrissie, who was passing out pencils.

"I know who I hope it will be," Chrissie said.

Bobby laughed. "Me, too, even if she is my mother."

The door opened, and Bobby's mother waltzed in, an elephant on tiptoes. Her folds and pouches shivered and shook, and her dark eyes twinkled. The Middles couldn't help reaching out to touch her rippling, rustling tent dress.

Emma Moore gave out a hug here, a pat there, then

sighed like an airplane tire going flat. "I do believe the only time you children learn anything is when *I* teach you. Well, let's make up for lost time." She tore pages out of a workbook and set the Middles to work.

She walked to the other end of the table, turned over a shopping bag, and poured out a dozen paperback books. "I begged, borrowed, and stole these," she whispered. That was probably true, Nell thought. Nobody owned much on The Farm, but the children had the least of all. The only books on the shelves in the dining hall were college texts and books on farming.

"Pick one and keep it for the week. Later you can exchange it for another."

Nell looked at *Little House in the Big Woods*. It seemed a little babyish.

"My favorite book," Miz Moore said.

If it was Miz Moore's favorite book, then it would be Nell's. She began to read while the Middles worked on subtraction. The clash and clatter in the kitchen faded away as Nell read about Laura and Mary and Ma and Pa. Ma did all the work in the house, and took care of the children all day long. That would drive Ilse right out of her mind, Nell thought. The Ingalls family lived in a much different world from the world of The Farm.

The dining hall door slammed. Tip stormed into the room with Hi Grady right on his heels. Nell couldn't remember when she'd seen her father so angry.

"I've put more time and work into this place than anyone! I'm not giving you anything else," Tip said.

Emma Moore flung up her arms. "I have a class here. Make noise somewhere else."

Hi Grady backed Nell's father against the huge fireplace. "You knew the rules of The Farm when you started. In fact, you helped draw them up. You can't break your own rules."

Miz Moore shook the hem of her dress at them the way she herded geese into the barn. The men did not notice.

"The money is for my family. It's in case this acts up again." Tip struck his head with his fist.

"Don't!" Nell screamed, worried that the metal plate in his head might break loose. She wanted to stand up and jump between the two men, but she didn't dare. The men glared at each other but did not raise their fists. Nell picked up her book and her jacket and ran.

2

The Willows' cabin had a small front room that had once been a porch, two bedrooms, and a bathroom with toilet and basin. The shower building was at the end of the row of cabins. Nell ran into her room, realized the book was still in her hand, and placed it next to an oak leaf pressed in plaster-of-Paris on a shelf Tip had made for her to keep her underwear and socks. The bed, pegs on the wall for clothes, and the shelf were the only things in the room. Nell sat on the bed and held her hands between her knees to keep them from shaking. "I could have saved him, if I hadn't been so scared," she scolded herself.

Tip's leg brace thumped against the floor of the front room, the door slamming behind him. "Nell, are you in there? Get Ilse. She's in the herb garden."

Nell grabbed her jacket and ran out again. In the cool, pale sun of late March, four women were planning the boundaries of the knot pattern for the herbs.

"Dad needs you."

Ilse dropped her ball of twine and strode ahead of Nell, so fast that Nell had to skip and half-run to keep up.

"He's not hurt or anything," Nell said through gasps for breath. "It's not his head. He's at the cabin."

Ilse led the way from the garden, past the dining hall, and down the road to the Willows' home. When they entered, Tip was pacing the front room. Da *dum*, da *dum*.

"What is it?" Ilse asked, not even winded from the brisk walk.

Tip's voice strangled away to almost nothing. "We have to leave The Farm."

Nell sank to the floor. Her fingers rubbed the boards, trying to hold on to home.

Ilse sat in a wicker chair. "Leave?"

He stamped his foot. "They want my money."

Ilse's skin paled to the color of skim milk. "Money? What money?"

Soon Tip would drill a hole and disappear.

"Sit down," Ilse begged.

Tip stuck his brace straight out and lowered himself to a metal lawn chair. "The money I have in an account for you and the girls in case this head blows apart."

"What money?" Ilse asked again. Now her breathing was ragged.

"When we started The Farm," Tip said, "we decided all money belonged to The Farm. If we earned anything, we would turn it over."

"I know, I know. Remember, I sold a poem and had to turn the money over to Hi Grady. But what money are you talking about?"

Tip spoke slowly and clearly, the way he did when talking to Abigail. "It was when you were having Nell in the Boston hospital. I had a headache, so I went to the Veterans Hospital for a checkup. They gave me some medicine. Something new they didn't know much about. It could help or kill me, they said. They also told me I was eligible for a disability pension."

"Why didn't you tell me?"

Tip shrugged. "Did you really want to hear that I might die? You were so happy with the baby."

Hearing that, Nell smiled, even though she'd rubbed a splinter into her palm.

"I decided to make sure you'd have money if that medicine didn't work. The government sends a check to the bank every month. That money does not belong to The Farm. It's for the plate in my head and the brace on my leg."

"I don't know how you kept a secret like that for so long," Ilse said. "And why did you decide to tell about it now?"

"I didn't." Tip spoke thoughtfully. "My bank statement came in the mail. I looked at it, then stuffed it in my pocket. It must have fallen out when I pulled my gloves out of my pocket. I didn't actually tell Hi, but I wasn't as careful as I usually am."

Ilse sat silently, as if the news was finally sinking in. "I remember the fuss I made about the poetry check. I refused to turn it over. I left The Farm and stayed two weeks with college friends. But this is different. We have two children now. We need to stay where someone else does the cooking and takes care of the children. My mother never taught me, and I certainly didn't learn how to cook in school. We're safe and comfortable here."

Nell agreed. Ilse could never play Ma Ingalls, and Nell doubted that Tip could plow a field without The Farm's tractor.

Tip's cheek twitched, a sign that he was upset. "I thought I'd lost you over that little check. I would have followed you, but I needed The Farm then. Now, I'm not so sure. I'll miss it, of course. All the friends we've made, the simple life here. But now it's looking more and more like a make-believe world, and I'm ready to go. The Farm has been a good place to live and to raise our girls, but we barely manage to survive. I'd like Nell to have a proper education and a library card. A place to sleep and food to eat isn't enough anymore. It's time we all went out into the world of books and music and a proper house of our own."

Nell did not want to hear about money or houses. "I don't care about money," she protested. "I don't want to leave." When no one paid any attention to her she stepped carefully over her father's outstretched leg and walked out the door.

She searched for the splinter while she walked back to the field of lambs. What if Tip went, and Ilse decided to stay? Nell tried to imagine living on The Farm with Ilse, or going out into a strange world of books and music with Tip.

The lunch bell rang, startling Blackie, who leaped to his mother's side. Nell dragged herself away from the lambs and headed back, obedient as always to the bell. Any

11

other day she would be handing in her books and papers and looking forward to a hot meal, but this was no ordinary day. She met Tip and Ilse on their way to the dining hall, where Abigail waited with the Wee Ones. Nell took Tip's hand.

"Won't you miss The Farm?" she asked her father shyly.

"If we go it will be because we have to," Tip said. "Of course I'll miss The Farm. But even if the Moores and the Gradys and all the rest feel like family, they're not. We're a family, and we're the most important thing." He looked down at her kindly as he tried to explain, and Nell felt comforted by his hand.

Tip kissed the top of her head. "Things might go rough at lunch," he warned.

What did rough mean? Fighting? "Don't come, Dad. I'll pick up Abigail and bring some rolls back to the cabin."

"No. There's no avoiding trouble. The sooner it's faced, the sooner it will be over."

"Will Hi hit you, Dad?"

Tip chuckled and squeezed her hand again. "Not with fists, but you can be sure there'll be some yelling."

The silence in the dining hall was as cold as a Vermont freeze. Nell's knees locked, as if she'd forgotten how to walk. Ilse picked Abigail out of the group of Wee Ones and held her on her lap at the table.

Nell sat on the bench between her parents, not quite sure who was protecting whom. She kept her eyes closed after grace, and listened to the usual sounds of soup, rolls, and fruit being served. She could smell lentil beans and ham. She opened her eyes.

The meal was a silent one with everyone looking at his own plate and none of the usual chatter. One last lentil rolled in Nell's bowl, but she stopped fishing for it when Hi Grady stood up, a dark shape against the south window.

"I'm sorry to tell all of you that Tip Willow has broken a rule of The Farm."

"What rule did he break?" Jim Moore asked.

"Money. Government money."

"Money" sounded terrible enough, but the word "government" made people's backs stiffen. Though they paid taxes and voted, most of the men still resented having been drafted, and felt the government had given them small support when they had returned from Vietnam.

Tip got up awkwardly and rested his good hand on the table. "That money is put away for Ilse and the children in case something happens to me."

Hi Grady had a quick answer. "If anything happens to you, The Farm will keep Ilse and Nell and Abigail, just the way The Farm would take care of my Chrissie and any other children I might have."

"You're lucky, Hi. You don't have shrapnel in your head that might come out at any time, like a splinter working its way through the skin. That money is kind of payment for my wounds. I intend to keep it."

"You know the rules, Tip. Sign the money over to The Farm, or get out."

Abigail wailed, as if she understood the angry words. Tip scooped her up from Ilse's lap and headed for the door. At the last minute he turned. "We'd appreciate a ride into town as soon as we're packed."

"Hey, good friend, let's talk this over," Jim Moore said, but Tip had already gone.

Nell packed her few clothes in an old suitcase, taking pants and shirts off the pegs slowly to give her parents time to change their minds. "You don't want to go, do you, Mom?"

"That quilt is ours. Roll it up tightly."

"Do you want to leave?" Nell asked again.

"No." Ilse sounded like she had a cold. "But I understand why Tip wants to. I sold a poem, and when the check came I wanted to keep it. Instead, I signed it over to The Farm. That hurt me."

Nell tucked her plaster-of-Paris oak leaf into the pocket of her robe. The only thing left was *Little House in the Big Woods*. She put the book inside her folded raincoat. I'll return it when we come back, she promised herself. No one leaves home forever.

She carried her things out and handed them to Tip, who packed them in the back of the van. The Moores stood watching. Ilse struggled with a cardboard box.

"My scribblings," she explained. "Twelve years of poems and journals." Tip covered the box, typewriter, and suitcases with Nell's quilt and then added Abigail's stroller, table seat, and other baby things.

"Say good-bye to Bobby and Chrissie for me," Nell said to Emma Moore.

There wasn't anything left to do. The cabin was empty, the van packed. Emma Moore hugged each of the Willows. "I feel like we're losing part of our family.

14

Keep in touch." She gave Nell a misty smile. "You can always come back, you know."

"We'll be all right," Tip said firmly. "When I came to The Farm I was still hurting. I'm better now." He herded Ilse and the girls into the backseat, then climbed into the front with Jim Moore. "Take care," he said to Emma.

"You, too."

"We're going?" Nell asked.

"We're going."

3

Nell braced her feet on the metal floorboard as the van bounced down the rutted road. Grown-ups left The Farm to buy food and seed, but none of the children had ever gone. As the van reached the gate, Nell held her breath. Tip got out to open the gate while Nell sat stiffly on the seat, not sure of what to expect. Was the air different in the outside world? Could children from The Farm live outside, or would they pick up germs or something worse that The Farm had protected them from?

Abigail squealed in The Farm's car seat, delighting in her first automobile ride. She hit the chair arms and swung her feet. Ilse stared out the side window, ignoring the baby's excitement. When Tip closed the gate behind them and got back in the van, Jim swung out onto the hard surface of a paved road. Nell took an experimental breath, then examined her arms and hands. Breathing was no problem, and she didn't feel any different.

They traveled through rolling countryside, heading downward toward a white spire that rose above the trees. Neat houses appeared at the side of the road and cars began to pass. Nell had just begun to think that the outside was beautiful, when they passed a field full of rusting cars, then an empty storefront, and finally pulled into a dirty service station with cars and trucks parked under whirling, brightly colored banners.

Jim parked under the flags, then he and Tip got out and began walking through the used-car lot. Ilse continued looking out the window, though there was nothing to see except gas pumps, and Abigail had settled her head to one side and closed her eyes. Nell opened the sliding door and closed it softly after her. She wanted to see everything she could on this first ride into the outside world.

"Are you looking for a truck or a car?" Jim asked.

Tip ran a hand through his hair. "I don't know. A truck, I think. If I can get a farm, a truck will be handy."

"Not much room for a family in the cab," Jim said.

"Once we get where we're going, we probably won't ride together very often. What do you think of this one?" Tip stopped by a dark blue truck.

"Looks to be in pretty good shape, though you can never tell. We'll have to take her for a drive." A salesman approached, an older man with cracked lips stretched into a smile. Jim said quickly, before the salesman reached them, "Any idea where you're going?"

Nell leaned forward to hear Tip's answer. She had wondered that all through the van ride.

17

"When I was a kid we drove up the coast from Boston and found a camp where we stayed a few days. There were small cabins and a dock, right on the water, in Maine. That was one of the best times of my life."

"Can I help you?" the salesman said, interrupting Tip.

While the men went about the business of testing the truck and filling out papers, Nell walked around, looking in car windows and thinking about Maine. A bubble of excitement replaced some of the morning's sadness.

Tip and Jim unloaded the van and piled everything in the back of the truck. Tip built walls of boxes and baby furniture around a corner behind the window, stuffing all the blankets and pillows into the empty space. "Your bed, Nell. Keep your nose down and stay covered up."

Jim moved the car seat from the van to the truck. "You'll need this. We'll get another one. We don't use it very often."

When the truck was ready, Tip reached out a hand to Jim, but what started out as a handshake ended as a hug. Nell's eyes smarted as she watched her father say good-bye to his friend. Tip had sounded so sure of himself when he said it was time to leave The Farm, but Nell could see it was not any easier for him than it was for the rest of the family.

Ilse climbed into the driver's seat, since Tip couldn't drive until special controls were installed. Abigail sat in her car seat between Ilse and Tip. The truck cab had room for everyone but Nell. She slipped into her bed in the back, keeping some blankets under her and some on top. As long as it didn't rain, she would be warm and comfortable.

When Ilse started the truck and pulled out onto the street, Nell judged the afternoon half gone. The fresh air cleared her head. So much had happened in one day. This was the first car trip Nell had ever taken, and she was determined not to miss a thing. She tried to picture a map of New England, but she had no idea how far away Maine lay.

Nell tapped the window often to point things out to Tip as Ilse drove them through the mountains of New Hampshire, but she fell asleep soon after they crossed the Maine line. It was not until morning that she realized she was no longer in the back of the truck. She had slept right through her first night in a motel, but she made up for it at breakfast in the coffee shop by eating a giant stack of pancakes smothered in maple syrup.

Later in the morning the air changed. Nell tapped the window, pointing to her nose, and Tip moved his mouth widely to say, "The ocean." The smell was new to her, and she ran over all the words she knew to find one that described it, but none of the words fit.

The Atlantic Ocean was very close; so close that when they left the highway and drove down the main street of Blue Harbor, suddenly there it was, smooth and glistening under the March sun. Nell shrugged off her blankets and sat upright in order to see the town. At the top of the hill, an island of grass separated two roads, one hugging the coast, the other going north. On the island a granite marker stood, surrounded by flags. Ilse drove past it too fast for Nell to read the inscription. On the right, two-story houses with flower boxes at the windows were built so closely together that Nell imagined the owners had to walk sideways to get to their backyards. Heavy brick buildings followed, containing stores and a library. Ilse drove the truck behind the IGA market to a parking lot, right next to the harbor.

"Wait here," Tip said. He walked toward the stores. Nell slid from the back of the truck and ran to the water. Lying flat on the rough concrete, she stretched until her hand reached into the harbor. Shock from the icy salt water ran straight up her arm.

Ilse changed Abigail, bundled her up, and put her in her stroller. They walked slowly around the parking lot.

"Will someone do our cooking?" Nell asked. Now that they were in Maine, she began to feel a little apprehensive.

"Of course," Ilse said calmly. "I know how to study, how to play tennis, how to write. I'm not planning to starve you children. I can learn whatever I have to learn."

"Wouldn't your mother let you learn?" Nell's grandparents had never been invited to The Farm, and neither Ilse nor Tip talked about them.

Ilse jerked the stroller around a corner. "My mother kept me so busy with studies and music lessons, I never had time for cooking." She sounded so irritable that Nell stopped her questions.

Tip returned a little while later with long sandwiches of crusty bread filled with meat, cheese, and shredded lettuce. Sea gulls wheeled overhead and a fishing boat unloaded its day's catch while they ate. Nell felt clean inside, as if all the cooking smells and wood smoke of The Farm had blown away.

After the girls had fed the last crumbs to the scrappy gulls, Tip and Ilse headed up to the business district. Nell pushed Abigail along the dock. The baby's eyes closed, but Nell tried to see everything. She looked into the fish-splattered inside of a boat, and saw a house that stood on stilts over the water. Then she walked up to the main street.

This time she headed for the other side of town, crossing a bridge over a river that raced to the harbor. To the left was a gas station and some houses. To the right there were stores, and above the stores were windows with curtains. Down at the corner stood a large square brick building. It didn't look like a house, and there were no signs outside. Nell couldn't imagine what it might be, but if they stayed in Blue Harbor long enough, she was sure she'd find out.

She pushed the stroller with its sleeping baby back down to the truck. The sea air made her feel as sleepy as Abigail. She wanted to curl up in her quilt and pretend she was back home.

"There's a house for rent very near here," Tip said in her ear. He put the baby in her car seat and folded the stroller. "We'll follow the agent."

4

Nell woke up in her own room the next morning. Pale sun touched the faded blue-and-white wallpaper that covered the walls and eaves and even the ceiling. The room's only window was in a gable facing the street and the meadows beyond. The windowsill wore hills and valleys of lumpy white paint. Where the paint had chipped she could see layers of yellow, green, and blue. It was a very old window in a very old farmhouse.

The stereo filled the house with music. Tip and Ilse had gone shopping the afternoon before and had brought home food and the stereo and a few records. The music almost made up for not hearing the breakfast bell.

Nell slipped out of her bed tucked under the eaves and ran across the floor. Someone in the past had painted the floor a dusky blue and spattered black, red, and yellow paint on it, creating little bumps she could feel with her bare feet. From her very first closet she pulled shirt and jeans. Soon she was running past her parents' empty bedroom and down the narrow stairs that hugged the side wall of the house. At the foot of the stairs, Nell turned right, past the front door, then right again by the front room and down the hall to the kitchen.

It was a square kitchen with a small pantry, and next to that was the house's only bathroom. A window over the high sink framed the pink eastern sky. Opposite was another window next to a big gas stove. Smack in the middle of the kitchen stood a plank table, scrubbed white after years of use.

Abigail sat in her little chair that hooked on to the table and hit her fists into her cereal. Nell was relieved to see that her mother knew how to make cereal. Maybe they wouldn't starve, after all.

A first ray of sunlight landed on Abigail, who shrieked and tried to grab it. Nell scooped cereal out of the pan and carried her bowl around the other side of the table so she did not break the ray. "What about school?" she asked.

Ilse drank her coffee and raised an eyebrow at Tip. "We thought since it's so late in the year, you might as well wait until September."

Nell felt relieved. She had no idea what a school was like outside The Farm. "Where is the school, anyway? What does it look like?"

Tip spoke up. "It was that big brick building at the corner of Main Street."

"A school is that big?" Suddenly Nell was delighted she didn't have to go to school. She took a lump out of the cereal with her fingers. Maybe there was a reason Ilse had not worked in the kitchen.

"What am I going to do all day if I don't go to school?"

"You'll help us. I'm going to do the farming. That's what I know best." Tip sounded very sure of himself.

"But how do you know what to do? At The Farm there was a big schedule on the wall that told you the chores. Now you have to tell yourself."

"That's what we're going to do today," Ilse said. "Plan our schedule and see what we need. Your job is to watch Abigail and do the cooking."

"Cook? Me cook? I've never been in a kitchen."

Tip swished coffee in his mouth and made a face. "I think you can do every bit as well as your mother," he said.

Her parents got up and left the dishes on the table. Abigail was covered with cereal. If it hardened, Nell thought, it would never come off, and Abigail might end up looking like Nell's plaster-of-Paris leaf.

Nell took a sip of Tip's cool coffee. The bitterness pulled at the inside of her mouth. How could they just get up and leave her? Miz Moore was probably just going into the dining hall and handing out papers. Nell wanted to go back and sit at a clean table with a clean piece of paper in front of her.

Abigail rubbed her face and began to cry.

Nell pulled out drawers until she found a new washcloth, then gently began to remove the sticky cereal from the baby's hair, face, neck, hands, and arms.

Nell closed the door to the hall, so she and Abigail were alone in the kitchen. She put the baby down to explore the dirty floor. It was the first time Abigail was without the company of the Wee Ones, but she didn't seem to mind and babbled softly as she tried to pull herself up on chairs and table legs.

Nell pushed pictures of The Farm out of her mind, and looked the kitchen over. She had always wanted to be a kitchen worker, and now she was one. She decided to clean up first and then think about lunch. She started on the dishes.

The morning seemed to last forever. Nell carried Abigail upstairs when she made the beds, then back down while she checked the pantry. There were no toys for the baby, so she put some cans on the floor for Abigail to roll around the room.

On the shelves were beans, flour, onions, potatoes, cans of lard, and cans of soup. The refrigerator had vegetables and fruit. There was nothing ready-made except the soup, but that was just what they had for lunch at The Farm, soup and fruit. The only thing missing were those hot rolls the children could smell baking while they did their schoolwork in the dining hall.

When Tip and Ilse came in around noon, soup bubbled on the stove, and a plate of fruit sat in the middle of the table. Ilse brought Abigail down from her nap and seated her at the table.

Tip was excited. "A whole field of corn. That's what I'm going to grow. I'll have to rent a tractor and hire someone to plow the field."

"Have him plow a garden plot for me," Ilse said. "I'll raise vegetables and herbs."

"Will you grow the herbs in that knot pattern?" Tip asked with a smile.

"By myself? I'll be lucky if I can make a few straight

lines. You were right. Parsley is parsley no matter what pattern it's planted in." Ilse might not be able to be perfect in Maine.

Tip sat back when the food was gone. "Great meal, Nell. Only I'm still hungry."

"There wasn't any bread, and I don't know what to do with all that stuff in the pantry," Nell said.

"I can't help you. I've never learned to cook." Ilse sounded proud. "I'll put my mind to it in the fall when the garden is finished. I can only do one thing at a time."

Me, too, Nell thought angrily. "Couldn't you buy some things that are easy to make?"

"Most of that ready-to-eat stuff is poison," Ilse said. "You never know what the manufacturers add. I want you to eat the same kind of food you ate on The Farm. Natural, healthy foods."

"Well, we've got to eat," Tip said. "Nell is our only hope. I'm going to make a list of things we need, seed and tools for the garden. I'll pick up a cookbook when I go out. Maybe we can all learn something."

Nell knew who would be the one to learn something. She would.

5

Nell spent the evening reading the cookbook while her parents worked in the front room. They unpacked the few books they owned, and Tip set the records on shelves. When they came into the kitchen for coffee, Nell sat at the table with a piece of paper in front of her.

"There's so much in this book, I don't know where to start. I wish they had a list of things an eleven-year-old could make. When I learned those, I could go on to the next list. But everything is jumbled up."

Tip sat next to her and sipped his coffee. "The first thing you can try is coffee. This stuff of Ilse's is lethal."

Nell found the coffee page and had Tip read the directions out loud while she rinsed the pot. Together they measured the water and coffee, and then timed it while it perked. The kitchen began to smell like the dining hall did in the mornings, making Nell feel homesick. The feeling vanished when she realized the kitchen workers would never have let her make coffee on The Farm.

Even Ilse smiled when she tasted the coffee. "All I ever made in the dorm was that instant coffee. You can show me how to brew this next fall," she said to Nell.

Nell beamed. Ilse was used to people doing things for her, and words like "thank you" were hard for her to say. Nell poured a little coffee in a cup and stirred in as much sugar and milk as she dared.

"Good," Nell said. "If you like coffee. I don't think I do. I'll stick to just smelling it."

Tip turned to the section on breads. "My mother used to make bread. So did the ladies in the kitchen on The Farm. This looks a little hard to start with. Why don't you try the biscuits, Muffin?"

He wrote down the page number, and at the side of the page wrote "baking soda." "I'll get this in the morning, and you can try biscuits for dinner. I'll do the rest of dinner tomorrow."

Nell hugged her father, and their dark curls tangled together. "I'll learn something new every day if you'll help me." She felt warm and important, sitting at the table, a cup of coffee in front of her, talking to her parents like another grown-up.

A few weeks passed before Nell dared to make the bread. She baked biscuits every day, but they were boring and didn't make good sandwiches.

Tip went over the bread recipes with her the night before. He listed "yeast" on his shopping list, and promised to get it first thing in the morning.

28

The next day Nell waited until Abigail was napping before she set the flour and yeast out on the table. She wished she had seen someone make bread, so she would know what it should look like. That had been a silly rule, keeping children out of the kitchen at The Farm. Nell mixed in the flour with both hands, hands that were soon coated with the stickiest mess she'd ever tried to handle. The recipe said to add flour until the dough was the right consistency, whatever that was. She kept adding flour, her arms got tired, and her hands grew to twice their size, they were so covered with dough. Then Abigail woke and screamed.

Nell tried scraping the stuff off her fingers as Abigail's cries grew more urgent. Finally she went to the sink to rinse off the dough. Now her hands wore a gluey glaze. She wiped most of it off on a towel and ran up the stairs.

Abigail's face was red right up into her blond hair, and she croaked hoarsely after all her screaming. Nell picked her up. "You have a terrible temper," she said. Abigail shook her head as if she understood. "You didn't want to stay up here all alone, did you?" Abigail shook her head again. Nell changed the baby's clothes, all the while leaving little pieces of dough on shirt and diapers. "Now you look like a snowman." Abigail shook her head and smiled.

Back in the kitchen, Nell placed the baby in her chair attached to the flour-covered table. Abigail reached out and grabbed a handful, saying, "Uh, uh," and shaking her head no. Nell washed her hands, dried them, and began mixing flour into the dough again. Abigail reached over, pulled off a sticky piece and flattened it in a cloud of flour.

Gradually the dough felt smoother. Nell turned it over

in the flour and pushed it down, then folded it again and gave it another push. A piece of Abigail's dough flew through the air and landed on Nell's head. With floury hands she reached up and plucked it out.

Finally Nell put the dough in a greased bowl and covered it with a towel. She put the bowl on the warm stove, then turned to look at the kitchen: the table covered with flour, Abigail covered with flour, and flour all over herself added up to one big mess. Sticky bits of dough stuck to the floor, the chairs, and her sneakers.

Abigail laughed gleefully, waving her arms and sending more dough flying around the room.

The dough had to rise for an hour. Already it was time for Nell to make lunch. She decided to heat some soup before cleaning up. A happy Abigail continued to play with the flour while Nell opened some cans.

Ilse came in the back door. She never said much, but now she said nothing at all. Nell turned from the stove and felt a clutching inside her at the sight of Ilse's mouth set in a tight line.

"I'm making bread," Nell said.

"All over the room?"

Nell laughed in spite of her mother's grim look. "Guess so."

Spring arrived late in April. Nell knew how to make a loaf of bread and how to roll out a pie crust. As she worked she sang to Abigail or talked to her. Abigail talked back in long sentences that made no sense.

When the housework was done, Nell pushed Abigail's stroller outside to Ilse's garden.

Ilse was raising five kinds of lettuce, green onions, and

a line of feathery green that showed where carrots grew. A local farmer had helped Tip plow the field and the dark, rich earth warmed in the spring sun. Soon it would be corn-planting time. Everything looked so neat that Nell admitted to herself that the Willows might make it in the outside world.

"Come with me, Nell," Tip said one morning in June. "I have to talk to the insurance man in town, and Ilse wants to clean up the front room."

Nell stretched out her arms as if shedding the harness that had kept her in the kitchen. "A holiday? Are you sure?"

Ilse smiled. "I promise to take care of Abigail. I *am* her mother, you know, and I can take care of little girls."

"She's got a temper," Nell said. "She pulls herself up now, and walks holding on to things. She probably could walk by herself, but she scoots around faster if she crawls. She can say a few words, too." She couldn't help feeling apprehensive. Ilse paid so little attention to things, she might forget that the baby was there. "Maybe I shouldn't go."

"Nonsense," Tip said. "I insist you keep me company. We'll pick up those submarine sandwiches and bring them home so Ilse won't have to make lunch."

Nell flew to her room to comb her curls, which now reached to her shoulders. She looked in the wavy little mirror. She hated seeing last year's slacks and shirt and was glad she couldn't see down to her faded sneakers. She'd wait until the corn crop brought in some money before she asked for clothes.

Tip tooted the horn from the driveway, and Nell raced down the stairs and out the door.

Nell sat proudly in the cab of the truck, which had been fitted with a special gear shift so Tip could drive. Tip shifted gears with his left hand and they backed out of the driveway.

"How far is it to school?"

"Let's clock it." Tip read off the numbers and drove slowly. Nell tried to keep her eyes on the miles, but they were drawn to the countryside. Soon the fields disappeared, and houses took their place. When they reached the island between the two roads, she had Tip slow down so she could read the granite stone marker, erected to honor veterans of World War I and World War II.

"Where's the Vietnam War, Dad?"

"Guess they haven't gotten around to that yet." He continued his slow drive through town, across the bridge, and pulled up in front of the large brick building which was the school. "One point five miles exactly. You can make that in less than half an hour if you walk, though maybe there's a bus."

Nell considered the building. "It's awfully big. Do you think there are enough children to fill it?"

"I don't know, but at least we won't have to pay to build a new school right off. I have to check on taxes and all that while I'm here. Why don't you get out and walk around? I'll be in the building across from the IGA. Meet me in front of the IGA in an hour."

Nell had very little idea of time, but figured that she would probably be hungry in an hour. She got out of the truck, suddenly feeling alone and frightened, and gave Tip a hesitant wave as he turned around and drove back over the bridge. The large double doors of the school, so silent and heavy, made her shiver in spite of the morning sun.

It was a blue Maine day, hot in the sun, but with a crisp ocean breeze. At the bridge she hung over the railing to watch the water swirl upriver. This surprised her, since the water had flowed down the first time she saw it.

"Tide's coming in," a friendly voice said.

She pulled her head up to look at the open face of a boy around her own age. "I thought rivers flowed into the sea."

"They do. But this is a tidal river. Farther up it's mostly fresh water, but here, near the coast, the ocean tide moves up for several miles."

"Oh." Nell looked the boy over. Bobby Moore was the only boy near her age that she'd ever talked to, and this one was not like Bobby. He was taller than Bobby, thinner, and with a shock of blond hair. "I'm Nell Willow," she said, not knowing what else to say.

"I'm Daniel Rhodes," he said, seeming to be as uncomfortable as she. "Are you just visiting, or will you be coming to school in the fall?"

Nell shivered again. "I guess I'll be coming to school, if I have to."

Daniel laughed. His teeth seemed too large for his mouth, giving him a wide grin. "I know what you mean. But you'll like it. I'll be in fifth. How about you?"

"Fifth?" Nell hadn't any idea what he was talking about.

"Fifth grade." He didn't add any word like "dummy," but Nell heard it anyway.

"I don't know. I've never gone to a real school before." She felt like a dummy.

33

"How'd you get away with not going to school? Were you sick or something?"

"I went to a sort of private school," Nell said.

"Oh. Well, if they don't put you back in kindergarten, maybe you'll be in my classroom, Nell Willow. I'll see you around, and watch for you the day after Labor Day." He left, sprinting over the bridge and down to the dock.

Nell felt warmer, the shivers gone. She knew how far it was to the school, one point five miles, and she knew someone who went to the school. Daniel somebody. His last name had slipped clear out of her mind.

She smiled as she walked past the dock, breathed in the tangy smell of the ocean, examined the inflatable beach balls in a store window, read some real estate ads displayed in another window, and met Tip outside the IGA. Blue Harbor wasn't half bad.

"I'm going to use the front room," Ilse said one morning in July. "I'll work there in the mornings and weed the garden in the afternoons."

Tip became very still, coffee cup held between the table and his lips. "What kind of work will you do in the mornings?"

Ilse twirled her long hair into a knot and pinned it up. "My scribbling. At college I always did my best work in the morning. Did I ever tell you how encouraging Professor Stephenson was? I had several poems printed in *The Review*. Don't forget that poem I had published while we were at The Farm."

Tip's cup hit the table. "The money you got for that one poem wasn't worth all the fuss. It seems to me both

34

of us should work together to get this place ready for winter. Wait until the ground freezes. Then both of us can do some writing. I have some things to write about, too. Things that have not been said about the war."

"Of course," Ilse said calmly. "You can use the front room in the afternoons. The corn and vegetables are all planted, and the government money will take care of anything we need."

Nell wiped Abigail's mouth and set her on the floor. She knew Ilse had not heard Tip's words about waiting for the first frost. Ilse did not hear anything she did not want to hear. Her mind was set on writing in the mornings, and that was what she would do.

Nell also knew that whatever Ilse did *not* do would be Nell's job. Nell had the permanent job of doing everything her parents didn't do.

6

The radio newsman announced that the children of Blue Harbor would return to school the day after Labor Day. Daniel had said that, too, so Nell guessed she had to believe it.

Nell's hands felt cold as she and Ilse made dinner. "You can't get along without me," she said to her mother. Nell put biscuits in the oven while Ilse cut up vegetables for a salad.

"Of course we can, though I certainly don't *want* to get along without you," Ilse said. "Just come right home after school."

"You're sure that brick building is the school?" Nell knew it was, but still needed to be reassured. How could there be enough children to fill that big building? "Where's Dad?"

"He's out looking over the fences. He's got his heart set on getting a cow."

"He can't milk one, can he? Only one hand is strong enough to squeeze."

"He can do anything he sets his mind on. Though I don't know about his writing. He had to learn how to read and write all over again after the accident."

Nell picked up Abigail and buried her face in the baby's warm, soft neck. How could her mother call that an accident? The only accident was that he hadn't died.

"Are you going with me tomorrow?" Nell asked. "Or is Dad?"

"Nonsense," Ilse said briskly. She held up a tomato and looked at it with pride before cutting it up. Her garden had done well. "We're going to be much too busy. I'll have Abigail to take care of, and I'm right in the middle of a poem."

"I'm not going," Nell said. "I can read and now I can cook. I don't need any more school."

"The first day is the worst," Ilse said. "After that it's easy. I wish I could go back to school again. When I was your age, every paper received an A. My mother was so proud of me."

Nell was sure Ilse's mother had taken care of the house and cooked the meals so her little girl could do her homework after school. Here it was nearly fall already, and Ilse still had not learned how to make coffee. Nell put Abigail down to play with the metal measuring cups, and wished that was what she herself could do. "I could stay home and make a cake," she said.

"You have to go. It's the law."

In the morning Nell examined her few clothes. She had no idea what children wore to public school, but she guessed it didn't matter. She couldn't put on something she didn't have.

Wearing clean jeans and a plaid shirt that felt tight in the shoulders, Nell gulped her cereal, then wrapped a peanut butter and jelly sandwich in waxed paper.

"Do you think there'll be something to drink there?" Peanut butter might stick in her mouth all afternoon.

"Don't know." Ilse didn't seem worried. She found a quarter and slipped it in Nell's jeans pocket. "That's in case they sell milk. Go to the office when you get there, and someone will help you. And don't forget to come straight home after school," she reminded Nell.

"Are you sure that brick building is the school?"

"If there's an American flag on the flagpole it is. Now, go."

The Willows' house stood so close to the road, two jumps took Nell to the street. She thought she remembered a yellow school bus passing last spring, but she had decided to walk the one point five miles. She had no idea what "point five," meant, but guessed the walk would give her time to prepare for her first day in a real school.

The fields of yellow and brown soon gave way to clumps of trees. The red and yellow leaves among the green reminded her of Vermont. She should be sitting at the table in the dining hall, listening to the clash and clatter of pots in the kitchen, waiting for the door to open and the teacher of the week to come through.

At first only a few houses could be seen through the

trees, small white houses with black shutters, set in the middle of green lawns. Nearer the village the houses stood next to each other, their window boxes still filled with summer flowers. Early settlers had built right down to the shore, and some of the houses stood on stilts anchored in the quiet harbor.

Nell forced herself to pass lobster pots, boats at anchor, and fishermen in high rubber boots. She promised herself that if she lived through this first day of school she would look at everything on the way home.

The Blue River cut the village in two. Nell crossed the bridge high above foaming water that swirled its way to the ocean. The tide is going out, she thought, remembering Daniel's words. An American flag waved in front of the two-story building ahead of her. Nell took a deep breath of salt air and hurried forward. A square of granite above the front door had the date 1903 carved on it, and beneath was etched BLUE HARBOR ELEMENTARY SCHOOL. The sound of young voices on the playground assured her that this indeed was the school.

Nell climbed the front stairs and pulled open one of the heavy doors. The polished floor smelled of lemon oil. The thundering of her heart echoed down the empty hall. She knocked softly on a door with OFFICE painted on the glass.

A round man wearing round glasses and a half-circle of a smile opened the door. Nell felt braver as she smiled back.

"What can I do for you, young lady?" the man asked.

"I've come to go to school."

"I'm the principal. Mr. Quimby." He held out his

hand for Nell to shake, but his attention was on the door of the office. He peered out into the hall. He looked puzzled when he turned back. "Where are your parents?"

"They're home," Nell said, feeling puzzled herself.

"It's just that new students usually come in with their parents. I don't think we've had one in all my years of working in schools who came in alone."

"Oh." Nell had hoped to slip into a seat and not cause any fuss, but now she knew that she was different, the only student to come in without her parents.

"Don't worry," Mr. Quimby said, putting a hand on her shoulder. "It's perfectly all right. I think you can give me all the information I need. Miss Mabrey, we have a new pupil."

The secretary smiled at Nell and handed the principal some papers. A bell shrilled, and Nell could hear the stomping feet of students entering the building. "Don't worry about being late," Mr. Quimby said. "You can go to class after we talk a little."

Nell followed Mr. Quimby into his inner office and was given a chair. The principal sat behind a big oak desk and took out his pen. "Your name?"

"Nell. Nell Willow."

"What grade are you in, Nell?"

"I really don't know, sir. We didn't have grades at The Farm. There were the Wee Ones, the In-betweens, the Middles, and the Big Ones. I was a Big."

His mouth made a round O. He reached behind him and pulled a book off the shelf. "Why don't you read for me?"

Nell smiled, and read:

"The morns are meeker than they were,
The nuts are getting brown;
The berry's cheek is plumper,
The rose is out of town.

"Miz Moore read some Emily Dickinson to us."

Mr. Quimby slipped the book back on the shelf. "How old are you, Nell?"

"I was eleven in February, sir," she said.

"Good." He went to the door and spoke to Miss Mabrey. "My secretary's calling the fifth grade. They'll send a student down for you. Your teacher is Mrs. Cavendish. She is fond of Emily Dickinson, too." He handed Nell a piece of paper. "Have your parents fill this out for you to bring back tomorrow."

The door burst open, and in pranced a tall girl whose straight brown bangs sat just above straight eyebrows. Her wide-set eyes glinted with mischief.

"Mimi, this is Nell. Take her back to class with you and see that Mrs. Cavendish lets you sit next to each other."

Mimi reached out a strong, brown hand and led Nell down the hall. "You'll love Mrs. Cavendish. She's tough, but she really keeps things moving. I hate to sit still and keep quiet, don't you?"

Nell nodded, though she wasn't sure, after a summer of quiet spent mostly in one room.

"The kids are nice. Most of them have been in this school since first grade. You'll like them, once you get to know them."

Mimi stopped her rapid-fire monologue when they reached the door with a large 5 painted on it.

The fifth grade room was cheerful and sunny. The desks formed squares of four, and the walls bloomed with red paper apples and yellow leaves. Nell looked around, her eyes drawn to the bright colors. Daniel sat by the window, and he raised his hand in greeting, his face split by a wide grin. Nell felt warm and comfortable, and she gave a shy wave back.

Mrs. Cavendish turned when they entered, and the first thing Nell saw was that she was old. Grown-ups on The Farm were all about her parents' age, so Nell had not been familiar with any older people. But Mrs. Cavendish's hand was firm when she greeted Nell, and her graying hair quivered with life. Nell decided in that moment that next to Miz Moore, Mrs. Cavendish was her favorite teacher.

When school let out at three, Nell knew many things. She was behind in math and ahead in reading. She had no idea of the geography of the world. The school served hot lunches and sold milk. The school in Maine had more books, paper, globes, and everything else than the school on The Farm.

Nell thought she agreed with Ilse that going to school was a wonderful thing. She would study and get all A's, like her mother had. She hated to go home.

"My house is down this road." Mimi pointed the way. Three younger children spilled out of the school yard and wrapped themselves around Mimi's legs. "These are some of the pesky little ones in my family. Maybe you can visit someday after school." She started moving, and the children untangled themselves. "Meet you here tomorrow morning," Mimi called over her shoulder.

Nell wanted to run with Mimi and join that noisy group, but she thought about Ilse. Ilse might be ready to tear out her hair after a day alone with Abigail. Reluctantly, Nell turned toward home.

Daniel fell in step beside her. His shock of straw-colored hair stood up like haystacks in the fields, and his eyebrows, bleached by the sun, were almost invisible, giving his face an open, startled look. "I'll walk you as far as my place," he said.

"Where's your place?"

Daniel matched his steps to hers. "You know the wharf where the lobster boats come in?"

Nell nodded.

"There's a house on the wharf, near the bridge side. We live there."

"How lucky you are." Nell remembered seeing the weathered house that first day in Blue Harbor, and could imagine the rise and fall of the tides, the slap of water against wood, underneath the house. That would sound better than the wind rustling the dying corn stalks in Tip's field.

"Mrs. Cavendish seems nice."

"She likes kids, that's why," Daniel said. "Teachers don't always."

"Do you have a boat?"

"Dad does. He's a lobsterman except when the temperature drops below freezing. Then he fishes."

"I never saw the sea before this summer. I've been trying to think what it smells like."

Daniel kicked an acorn across the bridge. "I dunno. Rockweed, fish. There're some days it smells like the inside of a clam bucket."

The inside of a clam bucket, Nell thought. She wondered if Emily Dickinson would describe the sea that way.

"The harbor isn't really the ocean. That's out farther."

Daniel turned toward the wharf. "Meet you here tomorrow at quarter to eight."

Nell rearranged the books she was carrying home and managed to wave a hand at him. She wanted to see Daniel's house and ask him more questions about the ocean, but if she didn't hurry, her arm would break off. Besides, Ilse might be bald already from taking care of the baby. Visiting Mimi and Daniel would have to wait for another time. She hurried through the town, past the monument, and out by the fields near her house. She couldn't wait to tell her family about her first day in a real school.

7

Ilse thrust Abigail toward Nell without a "hello," or "how was your day?". "*He's* supposed to watch her part of the day, but no, *he* had to take the truck some-where. I've been baby-sitting all day." She closed the door to the front room after herself. Nell felt relieved that her mother still had all her hair, but wished she'd had a chance to tell Ilse how much she liked school and how she was going to get all A's.

Nell dropped her books, lifted Abigail from the floor, then kissed her red cheek. It was easy to see from the puffiness of her eyes and the tear tracks down to her chin that Abigail had not been any happier than Ilse. "I'll bet you haven't been outside all day, have you?"

Abigail shook her head. "Out, out," she demanded, wriggling her way to the floor. Poor Ilse, Nell thought.

Abigail was no longer a baby one could leave in a crib. She needed things to do and someone like the Wee Ones to play with. Abigail stood still while Nell put on her coat, then she ran to the door.

Outside, Nell peeked in the front window. Ilse sat at her desk, staring at the typewriter. What had all that hurry been about?

In back of the farmhouse a picnic table sat next to a stone barbecue. Nell put the baby down on the many-colored leaves, then sat on the bench.

"What a great day I've had," Nell told Abigail. "Mimi's my best friend. Daniel's next to best. And Mrs. Cavendish is the greatest teacher. After Miz Moore, of course." Abigail put a red leaf in her mouth.

The Willows' blue truck drove up the two ruts in the grass that made their driveway. A V on the license plate showed that Tip was a disabled veteran. A second truck followed Tip. The driver put down a ramp and led a red cow off the truck.

"Her name is Rose," Tip said. Nell held Abigail up so she could scratch Rose between the ears. Rose had big, dark eyes and long eyelashes. The Farm had never had such a pretty animal.

"She's beautiful," Nell said.

Tip ruffled her hair. "Not quite the pet you used to want, but she's a good milker."

Nell looked fondly at her father. Imagine Tip remembering that she wanted Blackie for a pet. Now Blackie would be big and fat, just like his mother. Next spring he would be a yearling.

Tip led Rose to the fenced field. Nell wished she could tell him about school and ask him if he had gotten all A's when he had been a boy. But she guessed he could do only one thing at a time, just like Ilse. Nell gathered lumpy green apples from the apple tree by the back door, letting Abigail pick up the ones on the ground. It was one way of keeping Abigail from running after the cow.

Later, while Nell rolled out the crust for an apple pie, Abigail tottered around the kitchen, reaching for the apple peelings in the pail Ilse kept for garden compost, the soup cans in the pantry, and potatoes in the bin.

"Hurry and grow up, shrimp," Nell called over her shoulder. "I could use some help around here." Abigail grabbed a handful of flour and sifted it through her fingers to the floor.

Tip carried in a pail of milk. "No problem milking with one hand, it just takes twice as long. I'll show you how to pasteurize it. That can be your job. I've got to work on that shed before the cold weather so Rose can stay warm at night."

Nell watched carefully as Tip poured the milk into a large pot and heated it. She had to do it right, so she wouldn't waste Rose's milk. But inside her head was an angry voice that said, "Another job? Just what you always wanted."

"Why don't you teach Ilse to do that?" she asked. She knew it was wrong to question her parents, but she felt she and Tip understood each other.

Tip kept his face toward the milk. "Sorry. She's so involved with her poetry. Besides, I know you can do a better job."

Nell had no answer for that. She knew Tip was right. She tried to quiet the angry voice by thinking about Mimi. Mimi had lots of brothers and sisters, and probably had more jobs than Nell did.

October turned nippy. Frost sparkled on the yellow grass in the mornings, and Nell could see her breath as she walked to school. Tip had better hurry up with the shed. Rose had been with them a month, but the shed still had gaps in the walls and a leaky roof.

One Monday morning Mrs. Cavendish passed out small green notebooks. Nell opened hers to make sure she had it right-side up. The top line on each page was red, and the other lines were blue.

"Boys and girls, these are your journals. Your own personal property. Only you and I will see them. I may write a comment in the margin, but I won't grade them. When you come in every morning, write in your journal. Write down what you've been doing, your thoughts, anything you want."

Nell ran her fingers over the smooth cover, wishing she didn't have to spoil the notebook by writing in it. She watched Mimi draw her name on the cover with a felt-tip pen. Over each "i" she drew a neat circle. Nell tucked the notebook into her geography book without writing anything at all.

Ilse cried at dinnertime. "I don't know why I'm crying," she said, wiping her eyes on a paper napkin. "When we were on The Farm I was busy, and I had people to work with and talk to. Now I sit by myself in that room and have no idea if my work is good or bad."

Tip laid his fork down. "You want to go back?"

Ilse smiled a watery smile. "No. That part of our lives

is over. I think I'll write Professor Stephenson at the college and send him some of my poems."

Nell went to the stove for the coffee pot. It didn't seem right that cool, calm Ilse should cry.

"There's no reason our friends can't come here," Tip said.

"Jim and Emma Moore?"

"And Hi and Doris, if you'd like. Hi was rough on us, but he's still a friend."

Nell looked at her parents with delight. That trip from Vermont to Maine had been such a long one, she had never thought that someone might want to come from The Farm. Oh, she had so much to tell Miz Moore.

"Isn't it too far for them to travel?" Ilse had the same doubts as Nell.

"Not so far on the map, but with the mountains and all it took us about eight hours. Maybe they could stop at a motel like we did."

Ilse gave a short laugh. "Farm people don't have their own money to do things like that. Remember?"

Tip remembered. "Well, then, they'll have to leave early. Doris always got up early to start the kitchen moving. If they get on the road at four they should come in the driveway about noon."

"We'll serve one big meal and they can leave any time after that." Ilse started planning.

Tip phoned Jim and set the get-together for Sunday. Ilse shooed Nell out of the kitchen and, to the amazement of everyone, did the dishes herself.

Propped up in bed by two pillows, Nell wrote sentences for language and finished her math. Then she pulled the green notebook out of her geography and carefully printed NELL WILLOW on the cover.

On the red line at the top of the first page, she wrote *October 20*. Thoughts scurried around in her head. How did Ilse and Tip pick which thought to write? Anything that comes into your head, Mrs. Cavendish had said.

Everything came into her head. What if Ilse had said, yes, she wanted to go back to the farm? At the beginning of the summer, Nell would have been overjoyed, but now she was not so sure. Her cooking improved every day, school was a wonderful place to be, and she had more time with Abigail. She shook her head to clear it and decided to tell about her day.

I got up at six. I dressed. I ate oatmeal with maple syrup. I went to school. I came home.

Nell stared at what she had written. "I"s leaped up from the page. A whole army of "I"s. How boring. It had been a good day, except for Ilse crying, so how could it have been so boring?

She shouldn't have written in her clean, new book. If she tore the page out, the back page would fall out, too. Thank goodness Mrs. Cavendish was not going to grade the journals, or her plan to get perfect grades would have been lost already. She slid her journal back into the geography book and turned off the light. Tomorrow she would think more before she wrote.

In the morning, Daniel waited for her at the dock. "Pop went out this morning, but if this cold keeps up, the lobster season will be over early. The lines get ice on them and winds blow up from out of nowhere."

They fell into step, heads bent against the wind. "Don't you worry about him?" Nell said.

"Sure. Ma and I worry all the time. But that's what he does. It's his job. Don't you worry about your father?"

"I would have if I'd known him when he was fighting in Vietnam, but he's not in danger now, except for his head."

"His head?" Daniel's kind blue eyes looked bewildered.

"He's got a steel plate in it. Sometimes his head hurts."

"Oh."

Lobstering sounded dangerous, but Nell was sure Tip could do it. He and Daniel's father could go out in the morning and turn what they caught into money. Then, at night, Tip could write. Real fathers worked first and did what they wanted later.

In class, Nell sat at her desk and took out her journal. There were those "I"s again. Daniel was bent over his notebook, and Mimi was scrawling in hers. Nell sorted her thoughts carefully.

Maine cold is damper than Vermont cold, she wrote. *Lines on the lobster boats ice up and wet wind digs up my coat sleeves.*

She looked over what she had written. No "I"s this time. Now she had two "up"s.

"You're getting the idea." Nell covered her words with her arm, but she knew Mrs. Cavendish had seen her "I"s and "up"s. "The more you write, the easier it gets."

Nell felt like she had come to school with a hanger still in her shirt, and Mrs. Cavendish had slipped the hanger out.

8

On Tuesday, Nell went to school, her mind so full of planning for the Sunday visit that she couldn't think of what to write in her journal. She jotted down a list of what she had to do before the Gradys and Moores arrived.

> *Make two apple pies*
> *Bake two loaves of honey-bran bread*
> *Scrub the kitchen*
> *Mind Abigail*

She hoped Mrs. Cavendish wouldn't look at what she'd written, but the teacher had said she should write what was on her mind; and pies and bread were the most important, being the things most likely to please Ilse.

The day dragged on, filled with maps and commas. Nell was startled to hear Mrs. Cavendish tell the class to clear their desks twenty minutes before the dismissal bell rang.

"We're at the end of the first marking period," Mrs. Cavendish announced when everyone had settled down. "I'll pass out your cards and wait until you've had a chance to study them. Then I'll call you to my desk to see if you have any questions before you take them home."

"Cards?" Nell whispered to Mimi.

"Report cards," Mimi whispered back.

That must have been what Ilse had talked about. The ones she got all A's on. Nell breathed in deeply. What if Nell Willow didn't get all A's?

Mrs. Cavendish handed Nell a manila envelope with 'Nell Willow' written neatly in teacher's handwriting.

Nell held the envelope below desk level as she fumbled with the clasp. She drew out the card and looked at it, not understanding anything at first, then gradually she panicked. There wasn't an A on the card. Not one.

When Mrs. Cavendish finally called Nell to her desk, Nell gripped the report card with cold fingers and walked reluctantly to the front of the room. Mrs. Cavendish was her friend, and Nell felt she had let her teacher down.

"It's your first report card, isn't it, Nell?"

Nell nodded, still holding the offending card.

"I think it's a pretty good one. There are some areas you need to work on to make up for studies you've missed, but on the whole, you're an excellent student."

"Then why didn't I get any A's?"

"Because we don't give letter grades. If you look on the back of the card, you can see that the numbers mean certain letter grades. Now, you received a 97 in math. On the back you'll see that 90–100 is an A."

Nell let out a whoosh of air. Now she could see that she'd gotten at least three A's.

"Your geography background is woefully deficient, and I don't think you ever had science before. But I'm sure you can get those grades up next marking period."

"Yes, ma'am," Nell said with fervor. She put the card back in its envelope to study later. At least she hadn't disgraced the family too badly.

Willow was the last name, alphabetically, so Nell was the last to take her seat. "Carry your cards home and have them signed by your parents," Mrs. Cavendish told the class. "Please bring them back tomorrow. Don't let the dog eat them, or accidentally put them out with the trash. And don't try signing them yourselves. I know your handwriting."

Knowing the family would be scattered until dinnertime, Nell left the report card tucked in her journal on the bottom step of the stairs. As she walked to the kitchen, she worried about the list she'd written. Except for watching Abigail, she couldn't do anything else to get ready for Sunday. Nell was determined to show the Moores and the Gradys that the Willows were doing well. The shed worried her the most. A good farmer takes care of his animals, Nell knew, but Tip put Rose in the cold, drafty shed every night.

Tip came into the kitchen while she was peeling potatoes. He picked Abigail up and pretended to bite her fingers.

"More, more," Abigail giggled.

Nell hesitantly broke into their play. "If you have time, Dad, maybe you could work on the shed. Rose needs a warm place for winter." She didn't add that the visitors would see it, but she was sure that Tip understood what she didn't say.

Tip put Abigail down. "I know, I know. Things seem to overwhelm me. Your mother disappears into that room, and I'm alone. There's too much for me to do without help. If it weren't for you, we probably wouldn't eat a decent meal."

Tip sounded discouraged, and that frightened Nell. "Maybe I can help you outside."

He shook his head. "You do more than your share. You'll be making most of Sunday's dinner."

"I can't do everything on Saturday and clean up the kitchen, too. I think both of us need help."

"The women in The Farm's kitchen used to bake a week before a big dinner and then freeze the pies. We can do that, too. We'll defrost the pies Saturday night, and heat them up on Sunday."

Nell gave him a hug. "Thanks, Dad. I'll make the pies tonight. Are you sure there isn't something I can do for you?"

"I just need a push once in a while. I'll go right out and put a shingle on the roof. Give me a push, will you?"

She gave him a playful shove, and he took his jacket and went out the door.

———

After dinner that night, Nell knew she couldn't put off showing the report card any longer. It had to be signed and returned the next morning, and this was the only time the whole family was together. She went down the hall and pulled the card from her journal.

"We got our report cards today," she said, handing the envelope to Tip. She suspected he might forgive her for not getting all A's.

Tip clumsily removed the card from the envelope and looked it over with approving nods before passing it to Ilse.

"There are no A's," Nell said quickly. "On the back it tells what the numbers mean." She thought Ilse looked sad or disappointed as she ran her finger down the numbers and turned the card to see what they meant. Still her mother said nothing. Nell stood, waiting, her eyes only on Ilse.

"Only numbers," Ilse said. "I'm sure numbers are right for math, but how can Mrs. Cavendish give numbers for reading? Do they have numbers for understanding and appreciation?"

No one answered her question.

Tip smiled warmly. "I never got a report that good," he said. "You've missed years of schooling and you didn't even go to school for three months last year. You've done well."

Nell's back became straighter and her breathing more normal. At least one person wasn't disappointed.

Ilse continued to turn the card from one side to the other. "I'm sure if I got an A in math, it was closer to a 90 than to a 97. That math mark of yours is probably an A plus. I'm sure you don't take after me, Nell."

Nell wasn't certain how to take that comment. The

one thing she wanted was to be as perfect as her mother. But she didn't want to be better than Ilse.

Ilse took a pen out of her shirt pocket. "There's only space for one name. Do you want to sign it or should I?" she asked Tip.

"You sign it, Mom. Please." Nell watched her mother write her name slowly and carefully. A signature meant Ilse accepted the marks. Next marking period, Nell resolved, she would work harder on science and geography to bring her report card closer to Ilse's record of all A's and maybe make a few mistakes on her math homework to bring her math average down closer to Ilse's 90.

Early Wednesday morning, while Tip and Ilse were still drinking their coffee, Nell went out to check on Tip's progress. A bale of straw leaned against the shed. Next to the straw sat a pile of boards ready to cover the biggest cracks, and a large package of black shingles in big, rubbery squares. There was no glass to replace the broken window, and only a bit of shingle jutting from the roof showed that Tip had started working on the repairs.

That afternoon, the minute she got home from school, Nell dropped her books by the back door, then ran to the shed before Ilse could spot her and hand Abigail over. Nothing more had been done. She spread the thick, pale-yellow straw on the dirt floor. That would cut some of the cold that rose from the ground. She found a hammer and nails in the back of the truck and managed to cover some of the biggest holes in the walls with boards. Pa Ingalls would have fixed the shed before he got a cow, she thought as she banged angrily. Ilse heard the banging and called her in.

On Thursday Nell pulled one square of shingles from the package and, by standing on the pile of boards, managed to nail it on the roof next to the one Tip had put on. It was a small start and wouldn't impress Jim Moore, but it made her feel less worried about Rose. If she pushed Tip once a day and did a little herself each afternoon, Rose would be closed in before the snow came.

Warm sun slanted through the bare branches of the apple tree on Sunday. The early October frosts had vanished, and it was a perfect Indian summer day. That meant they could eat outside, instead of crowding around the kitchen table.

Emma stepped heavily from the van and nearly smothered Nell. "Oh, have I missed you! And you were just a tiny thing when your ma and pa took off," Miz Moore said, scooping Abigail high into the air.

Ilse's cheeks were pink as she welcomed their friends. "How was the ride?" she asked.

Emma laughed. "It made up for staying in one place twelve years. We left at four this morning. Even the animals were asleep."

"At least it was light when we went through the mountains," Hi Grady said. "I think I'll let someone else drive that pass on the way back."

After hugging everyone, Nell grabbed Emma's hand and pulled her through the kitchen, up the stairs, and into Nell's room. Shyly, Nell took a book off her shelf and held it out. "We left on the day you gave me this. I stole it."

"Oh, my, you have enjoyed it, haven't you." Emma

ruffled the well-read pages of *Little House in the Big Woods*. "It's yours to keep. There are more books in the series. I'll lend them to you when you come back." There was nothing Nell could say to that.

Ilse carried Abigail around as she pointed out the herbs in her garden. Great, dry clumps of basil with their pods of seeds marked the corners, and limp, yellow parsley hugged the ground. "You can see I haven't had time to tidy up," Ilse said, her voice high. Since Nell had started school, Ilse had given up her afternoons outside and had not cut the herbs to dry in bunches. The strain in her voice told Nell that her mother had been caught. Ilse, who wanted everything perfect, was being told on by her herbs.

Abigail wriggled to get down, but Ilse used her as a shield to cover her red face. Abigail became a thundercloud ready to burst, so Ilse turned her over to Nell and led Doris and Emma back to the picnic table.

Hi and Jim helped Tip with the fire in the brick barbecue. Smoke followed them around choking off conversation as they poked the wood and blew on faint sparks. Nell had never seen a man cook and wondered if the men knew anything at all about what they were doing.

Doris Grady sat stiffly at the table, her back to the men. Dark-haired and neatly put together, she ran the kitchen at The Farm. "I can't bear to watch," she said to Ilse. "Does Tip know how to cook?"

Ilse shook her head, the corners of her mouth twitching.

Emma reached for a piece of Nell's bread. "Your cooking has improved, Ilse. I remember that one and only day you worked in the kitchen."

"Nell does all the cooking, though I'm going to learn this fall. I write most of the day."

Emma faced the untidy garden and said, "That's nice," in a way that meant it wasn't.

Tip declared the meat done when it wore a thick, black crust. The Moores, Gradys, and Willows sat closely at the picnic table, passing bowls and platters of food around.

Nell brought out the second loaf of bread. "How're Bobby and Chrissie?"

"Fine, just fine," Emma said. "They wanted to come, but we don't often take them outside. Besides, it's a very long trip."

"Chrissie misses you," Hi Grady added. "I told her I was sure you'd all be back soon."

Ilse's hand shook as she sawed her clump of meat, and Tip moved his shoulders up tightly against the back of his neck. Nell held her breath. It wouldn't take much to blow this group apart if they kept mentioning a return to The Farm.

Apple pie and coffee eased the tension, but when Emma turned approvingly to Nell, Nell jumped up. The day had not been easy for Ilse. First the herb garden, then praise for Nell's bread. Ilse did not need to hear Emma compliment Nell on the apple pie.

"You haven't met Rose yet," Nell said. She plopped Abigail into the stroller and pushed her toward the field.

The only way to the field was past the shed. As the men neared it, Tip started telling about the acre of corn and the vegetables he and Ilse had grown. But talk could not cover the broken window or missing boards of Rose's shed.

Jim said mildly, "Not up to your usual workmanship, but I can see you've started."

Tip stopped in mid-step. It was the first time he'd noticed Nell's handiwork. "I suspect that Nell's the one keeping us going," he admitted. "Everything was easier on The Farm. We'd have worked on that roof together. Would have taken no time at all."

Jim was ready. "Get a ladder and we'll work on it now. It's the least we can do after that meal you served."

Yes, yes, Nell begged silently. Let them help. Come on, Tip, don't be so proud and stubborn.

Tip's shoulders were still tight against his neck. "No need to dirty your clothes. I'll get to it tomorrow."

9

The Farm was a different world, Nell wrote in her journal the morning after the cookout. *No one overslept, but if they did, someone else was there to take care of the children. I had many mothers and fathers, and the other children were my brothers and sisters.*

Nell put her pencil in the groove on her desk and thought about her morning and how different it was from mornings on The Farm. Instead of the clanging of the bell and the good-natured chatter in the dining hall, she had awakened in a cold, quiet house. A dismal rain pitted the windows but did not waken Tip and Ilse. Even Abigail lay sleeping, bottom rounded up, in her crib.

Nell crept out of the house carrying a piece of bread left from the day before, as well as her lunch, a sandwich of burned meat. Now she sat in the comfort of the schoolroom next to Mimi, whose long hair covered her face as she wrote. Mimi plunged into everything with a ready smile. Nell wished she could write more about The Farm, but her mind kept returning to the cold, quiet farmhouse. Had anyone wakened? Had Rose been milked? Was Abigail hungry?

The rain stopped before recess. Nell and Mimi held hands and ran to a jumble of rocks at the edge of the playground. The thick fog swirled around them, smelling, as Daniel had said, like the inside of a clam bucket.

Mimi climbed on top of the highest rock and stood facing the wind, a sea gull on a piling. "Come home with me this afternoon. Mom's making gingerbread, and there's something I want you to see."

Nell thought about her own home. Maybe everyone lay right where she'd left them. Just thinking of that cold, silent house made her tired. "I should go home, but I don't want to. I'd like to walk all the way back to Vermont."

"Don't do that." Mimi laughed. "My house is closer. And the surprise will make you feel better. Mr. Quimby will let you call from the office."

They ran in before the bell to make the phone call. Nell had never used a telephone before, and found she did not know her own telephone number. Miss Mabrey found it on the paper that Ilse had filled out, and Mimi helped Nell dial.

Ilse answered. In the background, Abigail jabbered, and Nell could not hear Rose bellowing. At least the family was up and moving around. Nell spoke fast, promising she'd come home as soon as she'd seen Mimi's surprise. She hung up quickly before Ilse had a chance to say no.

The village formed a big U around the harbor. Daniel lived at the very center of the bottom of the U; Nell lived off in one direction and Mimi in the other. When the dismissal bell rang, the girls hurried down the street toward Mimi's house. Mimi walked on the stone wall by the road, balancing, teetering, leaping over gaps. To the left of the wall, sea marsh stretched to the harbor.

"Are there any snakes here? Vermont has snakes in the stone walls."

Mimi grinned back. "Of course. Snakes and giant spiders and all kinds of poisonous things."

Nell shivered with delight. Chrissie would have said, no, there were no snakes; but Mimi would imagine snakes even if they weren't there.

"Here we go-o-o." Mimi leaped off the wall and darted across the road.

Mimi's house, white like most of the houses in Maine, sat back from the road with a large tree branching over the roof. A porch stuck out like a fender in front. Mimi leaped the porch stairs, two at a time.

Abruptly they were in a tidy front parlor so unlike the front room at Nell's house. Not a book or paper could be seen. Even the children's toys stayed in the dining area, as if all activity stopped at the living room rug.

"Mom, we're home," Mimi sang.

Round and flushed, Mimi's mother smiled a broad smile. "Nell." She wiped her hands on a towel and wrapped an arm around Nell's shoulders. She put her other arm around Mimi.

"How was school today, girls?" she asked.

Nell wished she could stand there forever, feeling warmly welcome, sniffing delightful smells of yeast and ginger, but there were others to meet. Mimi pointed them out. "That's Brad, and the one with the truck is Dave. Carla and Jen are at the table, and Amy is in the corner with the surprise."

The surprise was a small sheltie lying on her side in a box. Six glistening puppies nursed greedily. Amy held up one of the pups. It was black with white and gold markings, and it smelled of wet newspapers.

Nell held out her hands and cupped the warm animal so only its face showed. "I love it," she said, rubbing her cheek against the puppy's nose. "I've never had a pet. Have you homes for all six?"

"We haven't started looking, yet. They have to be at least six weeks old, and these were born Saturday." Mimi gave Nell a long look. "We'll save this one for you, if you think you can take it."

Nell put the puppy back on its mother's stomach. "I'll ask." She thought of the dog Jack, protecting the Ingalls family from Indians and wolves. A dog might be just what the Willow family needed.

"Sit, sit," Mimi's mother said. "We have gingerbread and fresh milk. You have a cow, Nell?"

Nell nodded as she took off her coat. The chair was covered with crumbs, but she sat on it anyway. "Where's your father?" she asked Mimi.

"At the shrimp-processing plant. He works there until after dark."

What a nice family, Nell thought. A mother in the kitchen, a father who worked, children and puppies all over, and the best gingerbread Nell had ever tasted.

Mimi walked Nell back as far as the school. "Walked" was not quite the right word. Nell showed how Blackie leaped stiff-legged, and Mimi followed behind her, imitating the antics of the lamb. Nell hadn't had such a good laugh in six months and soon flopped down at the side of the road until her breath came back and her ribs stopped aching. Mimi held out her hand to pull Nell up, and they tried to walk soberly, only to explode into giggles again. As Nell crossed the bridge, she looked back and saw Mimi leaping toward her home. Nell half walked, half ran the one point five miles with a smile on her face the whole time.

"That's the end of that," Ilse said coldly when Nell came in the door. "From now on you're to come straight home from school. It's dark already. Your father's out milking Rose and I've been stuck with the baby all day."

Nell's smile disappeared. She took Abigail into the kitchen, washed her face, and handed her a cracker before looking around for something to cook for dinner. She found some potatoes to bake and then started a batch of cornbread. Not a very balanced meal, but the refrigerator was empty.

Tip came in with the milk. "Hey, here's my girl. It's good to have you home. Your mother's been fussing all afternoon." He poured the milk into a big pot and rinsed the pail.

Nell carefully placed the pot on the stove. "How did your day go?" she asked.

He gave her a wide grin. "I have a good section written. It's all about this guy who went into the service right after high school. Like me."

"What else is for dinner?" Tip asked later, when he had finished the baked potato and the square of cornbread.

"I'm sure I don't know," Ilse said. "Things don't run right when Nell plays hookey." She walked out of the kitchen and into the front room, and soon the typewriter clattered.

Tip picked up a dishtowel and handed one to Abigail, who dried the spoons before banging them on the floor. Nell always washed them again after her sister was asleep. "Don't know when it's going to soak in, Nell," Tip said. "If I don't do something, like the shopping, it doesn't get done. Guess I'm a slow learner."

"That's okay, Dad. But we'll need something for tomorrow. Do you want to help me make a list?"

"Tell you what. You sit down and write, and I'll finish up these dishes and think what I'd like to eat tomorrow. Maybe I can get to the IGA before it closes."

Nell looked around for a piece of paper, but there was none in the kitchen. "Think I can bother Ilse for some paper?"

Tip flung out his arms, almost losing a cup. "Even *I* am not brave enough for that. I wish there were some way I could bring that woman back into this world, but I guess we'll have to wait until she gets this writing out of her system. See if there's a blank page in the back of the phone book."

While Nell made out the list and Abigail banged her spoons, Tip cleared the sink and drain board. "Just hang in there," he said to Nell. "Your mother will come back to the family someday." A sad note in his voice reminded Nell that he missed Ilse as much as she did.

This was not the best time to ask about the puppy. It was not a good time to tell Tip about the Tompkins family, either. Tip did not need to hear about a mother who watched her children and kept them well fed, or about a father who got paid for working a regular job. She would try another day, after Tip had eaten a decent dinner.

10

All week, Nell thought of the puppy. Each time Mimi asked her if she could take the puppy home, Nell had to say she didn't know. "But please, please, save that one for me. It is a boy, isn't it?"

Mimi nodded. "He's the best of the litter."

"I'm going to name him Jack, so you can call him that. Don't worry. I'll get him."

The last class of the day was interrupted by Mr. Quimby on the intercom. "Good afternoon, girls and boys. As you know, tomorrow you're expected to come to school dressed up. Please wear something that won't be too uncomfortable and won't trip you on the playground. I would prefer you don't wear anything on your face. The room-mothers have taken care of the parties for each class. Teachers, please save the last half hour for cleanup. We don't want to lose our custodian."

Nell was bewildered. What was that about wearing something on your face? Did Maine kids wear makeup when they dressed up? She turned to ask Mimi to explain, but the dismissal bell rang and Mimi shot out of her seat.

"Gotta go. Mom's taking us all to the store for stuff to wear. See you."

Nell dragged her feet on the way home. Dress-up day, and all she had were her jeans and old shirts. On The Farm the mothers went out twice a year and bought all the children's clothes, and outgrown clothes were passed down to smaller children. But this year she had nothing new to wear, and certainly nothing that could be called dressy.

She walked slowly past the small shops on Main Street, peering in to see if girls' dresses hung there. There was a pale-blue dress in The Smart Shop window that she liked. Was Tip's government money enough to buy new clothes?

Once past the town, she shuffled through dry leaves, trying to figure out her new problem. She hadn't dared to ask for Jack. Now she had two things to ask for, and she was quite sure if she asked for two she'd get nothing.

Most of the children in her class wore the same jeans and shirts that she did. The only difference was that she had worn through one knee in her jeans, and her shirts kept her from swinging her arms, they were getting so small. She kicked a horse chestnut and decided. A dress first, and Jack second.

Nell stood outside the little house, trying to summon up her courage. She would just have to march in and tell Tip how important a new dress was. She was so certain that Ilse would be deep in her own thoughts that she considered Tip her only hope.

When she opened the front door, Abigail flung herself at Nell and wrapped her arms around Nell's holey blue jeans.

"Hey, Sweetie, let me put my books down first." Nell dropped them on the bottom step, swung Abigail up in the air, then, still carrying the baby, went looking for Tip. He was not in the kitchen, but Ilse was there, heating the kettle for a cup of tea. "Where's Dad?"

Ilse put a tea bag into a cup, then sat at the table. "I'm glad you're home. Tip went out to get the truck tuned up and to buy some groceries."

Nell went to the stove as the kettle began to whistle. This was a bad turn of events. *Now* Tip had to remember to get groceries. Now, when she needed him the most. She poured boiling water into the cup and set it before Ilse. "Mom, I've got to talk to you, then."

Ilse flung her arms out, as if to say she gave up. "Two minutes, and then I'm taking the tea into my room. I finished a poem today. Don't ask me how, with that little one running around."

"Mr. Quimby said tomorrow's dress-up day. I don't have a dress. I don't have any clothes that fit or don't have holes in them."

"I never thought," Ilse said. She sipped her tea, a remembering look on her face. "When I went to college, I had two trunks of clothes. Sweaters and skirts and blazers. And a fine dress-up dress for concerts and teas."

A warm feeling filled Nell. She would get her clothes. All that worry had been for nothing.

Ilse put her cup down. "If I went to college with two

trunks of clothes, my daughter should have clothes for the fifth grade. I don't know if we can find anything decent in Blue Harbor, though."

"I saw a blue dress in The Smart Shop," Nell said. "The only thing is, it won't look good with sneakers."

"No. We didn't buy you shoes for school. Abigail hasn't any shoes at all. Where's my mind? Give me a few minutes in my room, and when your father gets home, we're going shopping."

The four of them drove to town in the truck, with Nell in the back. She didn't mind being cold if it meant clothes for dress-up day.

Ilse examined everything in The Smart Shop, talking constantly. This was not like her. She said things like, "I had a plaid skirt, so you should have a plaid skirt. And a navy-blue sweater." It was as if Ilse was filling her college trunks all over again.

As a final triumph, Tip picked up some of those long sandwiches they all loved. "No need for you to cook tonight, Nell. You'll have enough to do, putting your new things away."

Tip seemed happier than he had been in a long time, Nell thought as she hugged her box with the blue dress in it. For the first time the Willows appeared to be a whole family. She wished Mimi and her mother had been shopping in The Smart Shop. Then she could have said proudly, "This is my family."

Nell rose early to take a bath, shampoo her hair, and put on her new blue dress and shiny shoes.

"Don't you look nice," Ilse said, her voice surprised, as if she hadn't seen Nell in a long time.

"I love it," Nell said.

"Are you sure you can walk in those shoes?" Tip asked. "I can drive you to school."

Nell shook her head. "These shoes feel wonderful. I'll meet Daniel at the wharf. We're going to have a party at school," she told Abigail. "I'll try to bring something home for you."

Abigail had never seen a party, but she smiled anyway.

Nell wore the new winter coat Ilse had picked out. The wind whipped in from the ocean, and she wrapped the coat tightly around her. She felt warm inside. So much had changed since the day before.

Someone stood on the wharf. Someone about the same size as Daniel, but who wore a loose suit stuffed with straw and a big straw hat on his head.

"Daniel?" she asked. "Is that you?"

"I'm the scarecrow," the boy said. "Who are you?"

"I'm Nell," she said. "Don't be silly. We can't stand here in this wind. Are you going to school looking like that?"

Daniel smiled, wrinkling the freckles painted on his face. "I know you're Nell, but who are you today?"

Nell had the feeling that the world was not quite right. "I'm Nell, dressed up." She opened her coat to show off her new blue dress. "Mr. Quimby said this was dress-up day, and I'm dressed up. All new, too." She held up one foot to show off the shiny shoe.

"Dress-up means dress in costume. Haven't you ever heard of Halloween?" Daniel peered at her through bits of straw slipping out of his hat.

Nell shifted her feet uncomfortably. She thought she

might have read about it, but they had never had Halloween on The Farm. "You mean I'm all wrong?" She felt tricked out of her happiness. Why hadn't Ilse or Tip mentioned it? Some of the store windows on Main Street had been decorated with strange things, and they surely should have known.

"I can't believe you've never heard of Halloween. Where was that private school you went to, anyway? On Mars?"

Nell looked at her feet.

"Well, you can't be Nell. You have to be someone else, or something else on Halloween." He looked her over. "I know. You could be Dorothy. I know she wore a dress and had some shiny magic shoes. Hold on a minute."

The damp wind nearly froze Nell's tears before he came back from his house. "Here's your basket, and Toto." He handed her a basket with a stuffed dog in it. "Now you're Dorothy, and we're off to see the wizard." He swept Nell up the street and into the school.

Mr. Quimby walked the halls in a clown suit. Mrs. Cavendish wore a long black dress and carried a broom. Mimi had whiskers pasted to her face and a long tail trailing behind what looked like pajamas.

The room was draped with strips of black and orange crepe paper, and black cats arched their backs on the bulletin board. Nell found it hard to do division when ghosts and pirates went up to do examples on the board.

"What *is* this?" Nell asked Mimi when they stood outside during recess.

"Halloween," Mimi said. "Haven't you ever had a Halloween?"

Nell thought. "No. I've read some stories about it, but I never knew when it was."

Mimi looked at her as if she was crazy. "I've never heard of anyone who didn't know about Halloween. Are you sure you lived in this country before you came to Blue Harbor?"

Nell laughed. "Only if Vermont is part of this country." Her geography still was not very good.

Nell and Daniel walked over the bridge together after school. His straw was almost all gone, but his freckles were as bright as ever. "How'd you like your first Halloween?"

"It was all right. But I felt bad about not knowing. Thanks for saving my life." She handed him his basket and stuffed dog.

"Want me to keep them for next year?" he asked.

"No. Next year I'm going to be the weirdest, most gruesome creature you've ever seen. Monday is a regular day, isn't it?" She had to be sure she didn't make another mistake.

"Back to the old jeans," he assured her.

Nell's coat didn't seem as warm on the way home as it had when she started out in the morning. She walked briskly, thinking about how kind Daniel had been. He was sort of like Tip, she decided. Unfortunately, today she liked Daniel more than she liked Tip or Ilse.

Ilse met her at the door. "How did the class like your new dress?"

Nell pulled a crushed cupcake out of her pocket and handed it to Abigail. "I thought dress-up meant to *dress up.* I should have gone in my old clothes. Today is Halloween."

"Halloween? We decided there wasn't time for Halloween on The Farm. I haven't thought of it for years."

"Didn't you notice all the decorations in the store windows last night?"

Ilse looked at her sharply. "I was so busy remembering those wonderful days when I was in college, I hardly noticed anything else."

"Daniel helped me so I wouldn't look silly. He lent me a basket with a stuffed dog in it. He said I was Dorothy and the dog was Toto. I never heard of them, but all the other kids knew who I was."

Ilse stopped at the front room door. "You have a library at school. Go find *The Wizard of Oz.*" She closed the door behind her.

Nell took Abigail upstairs while she changed into old clothes. "Go find *The Wizard of Oz,*" she mimicked her mother. "I'll find it, all right. But how can I find the time to read it? That's what I'd like to know." She hung Dorothy's blue dress carefully in her closet.

11

School let out at noon the day before Thanksgiving. Nell waved good-bye to Mimi, and left Daniel at the wharf. She wished she could spend Thanksgiving in Mimi's house, which overflowed with children and dogs, or in Daniel's house over the water. She thought of the women in The Farm's big kitchen, baking pies and cooking sausage for the stuffing, and wished she was there. She wanted to go somewhere else for Thanksgiving, anywhere but the farmhouse.

Walking as slowly as possible, she still arrived home early in the afternoon. Ilse's brief spell of talking, the evening Nell got her dress-up dress, had ended the next day. Since then, Ilse seemed more unhappy, and sometimes Nell found her mother in tears.

Tip, too, talked less. Nell knew he worked on his book

while she was in school, and that Tip and the truck were often gone when she came home. The shed had not been touched, but he brought in Rose's milk twice a day and kept the refrigerator stocked with food, so Nell assumed everything was as right as it could be.

Nell opened the front door quietly and found Ilse running down the hall toward her. "The mail came at eleven and I've read this a thousand times. Your father has gone somewhere, as usual, so I haven't been able to show it to him. Here. You read it." She thrust an envelope into Nell's hand.

It was a letter from an editor in New York who was happy to send Ilse Willow a check for a poem called "Spindrift," and asked to see more of her work.

Nell hugged her mother and got a hug back. A letter a day from New York would mean a hug a day. "Where's the check?" Nell asked.

Ilse waved an arm. "On my desk. Single poems don't bring in much, but it's a start." Ilse danced around the hall. Abigail began dancing, too.

Nell heated up stew from the day before and was making a salad when Tip came in lugging the Thanksgiving turkey. Ilse barely gave him time to drop the turkey on the drainboard before she waved her letter in front of him. He wiped his hands before he read.

Tip's dark eyebrows almost met across the top of his nose the way they did when a window stuck, and his lips stretched over his teeth in a false smile.

"That's wonderful, Hon." Nell could barely hear him.

Ilse folded the letter and tucked it back in the envelope.

"You should be dancing around the kitchen. It isn't every day a person gets something accepted."

"You're right. The letter is truly exciting. But my dancing days are over, I'm afraid," he said, patting his brace.

A pang twisted through Nell. Tip rarely mentioned things he could not do. If he were truly excited, he could hop a few steps around the table. He looked almost disappointed, as if he had hoped Ilse would not do well with her writing.

"Nonsense," Ilse snapped. "The way I understand it, you never did much dancing, not in high school, and not in Vietnam. You should be glad that my time in the front room has not been wasted."

"I would rather have you taking care of the girls and helping out in the house. Those herbs of yours are frozen black and useless. Abigail needs more attention, and Nell could use some free time."

Tip and Ilse never argued, at least not in front of Nell. The raised voices excited Abigail, who had stopped dancing, and now she ran on tiptoes, her arms out for balance.

Nell slammed the oven door to remind them she was there.

"Why don't you take a walk?" Ilse asked sweetly.

The sky had turned dark, the air crisp. Nell raced across the corn stubble to the stand of pines and looked back at the house. The kitchen windows glowed, warm, yellow rectangles in the growing darkness. The farmhouse should have been a loving place, but it wasn't. Something was wrong.

That evening, Nell took down her cookbook. "I need help with this," she said to Tip. "I've cooked chicken, but I can't even lift a turkey."

Tip sighed. "There are times when I'd like to go back and let Doris Grady handle the dinner. I don't think your mother has even cooked a chicken, so that puts you in the position of being head chef. You take notes, and I'll tell you what we're going to do."

Nell found a piece of paper and a pencil. From the sounds of typing in the front room, she knew that Thanksgiving dinner would be up to her and Tip.

Tip ran his hand through his curls. "So much work. We should have started last July. The stuffing alone would take me a day—cutting up celery and onions, making bread crumbs, cooking sausage. Then there's gravy, and a pie. And we must have vegetables."

Nell sat with the pencil in her hand, waiting for directions, but Tip mumbled on about how impossible the whole thing was. Nothing would get done if all he did was ramble on. He put down the cookbook, and walked quickly to the door of the front room. He opened the door and the typing stopped.

Nell strained to hear, but as the voices rose the stereo went on loud enough to rattle dishes in the kitchen. Beethoven's Fifth drowned out whatever was being said. *Dum dum dum da*, the music roared.

After a few more bars someone turned the music down. Tip came back down the hall, Ilse at his heels. Tip looked at Nell's face, and laughed. "It seems we have a helper in this adventure. Write an 'I' for Ilse. Under that put 'cut up onions and celery, make bread cubes.' "

Nell wrote. Tip waited until she finished, then said,

"Write a 'T' for Tip. Under that put 'simmer giblets, cook sausage.' And as for you, my girl, write an 'N' and write 'bake pie' under it."

Ilse went into the pantry to get the onions, giving Nell a chance to ask, "How—?"

Tip leaned over and whispered in her ear. "I just said that we couldn't manage, and I was thinking we ought to give up and go back to The Farm. That check she got today was sitting on the desk. Your mother will do anything to keep from having to turn that check over to Hi Grady. And anything includes chopping onions and celery."

Abigail had run herself down and, unnoticed, crawled under the table and fell asleep. Working separately in the same room, Tip and Ilse simmered down, like the giblets and neck that simmered on the stove.

Thanksgiving dinner was much better in Maine than it had been on The Farm. With only four of them, chances were one could get the part of the turkey one liked. Nell chose the drumstick and worked her way through the strings of meat and the little sticks of bones, right down to the drumstick itself. Abigail mixed mashed potatoes with gravy and cranberry sauce, carrying the pink-brown mixture on a spoon that often turned over before reaching her mouth. Ilse kept exclaiming over the stuffing, as she had done most of the work. "Though you did a marvelous job with the sausage," she said to Tip. Tip put his hand on Ilse's, which to Nell was the best part of Thanksgiving.

I ate and ate and ate, she wrote later in her journal. *No one fought. Abigail could barely waddle after dinner and had to have a bath before she went to bed. Ilse helped with the dishes and did not go into the front room once the whole day. I thought about asking if I could have Jack, but the day was so nice I didn't want to ruin it.*

The day after their first Thanksgiving dinner away from The Farm, Nell took the mail from the mailbox. There were six manila envelopes, all addressed to Thomas Ian Philip Willow. She looked at them before taking them in. They had return addresses of New York and Boston, written in Tip's unsteady handwriting.

That's what had been wrong the day Ilse had gotten her check. Tip had sent out *his* writing, and it was coming back to him. They were both trying to get their work in print. That meant rivalry in the front room, and so far, Ilse was winning. Reluctantly, Nell carried the mail into the house.

12

Christmas was only two weeks away. A light snowfall in the night barely coated the stubble in the fields, leaving the ground a patchwork of white and brown. Nothing changed inside the house. There were no presents being wrapped, no decorations hung, no cookies sprinkled with colored sugar. Ilse sorted papers at the kitchen table, while Tip worked in the front room. Their battle was on full-time, though somehow Rose got milked and clothes were washed.

Nell talked to Abigail as she cleaned up the kitchen or cooked dinner. "Remember Christmas? We had it last year on The Farm. There was a big tree with lights on it."

Abigail shook her head. "Light," she said, pointing to the kitchen light.

"Santa Claus came into the dining hall. He wore a red suit and we got presents," Nell went on. True, they hadn't gotten much, but the handmade things had been wrapped and put under the tree. With so many children, the pile of gifts had seemed overwhelming.

"Presents," Abigail said. She didn't know anything. If no one talked to her and told her things, how was she ever going to learn?

In math class, Nell missed a step in multiplication. Had Tip and Ilse forgotten Christmas? On The Farm, the children made decorations for the tree early in December, and the women in the kitchen baked for a month.

That night Nell pricked halves of acorn squash with a fork as she prepared their dinner. "Have you thought about Christmas, Mom? It's less than two weeks away."

Ilse tossed a strand of hair off her face. She seemed half asleep. "Christmas?" Her voice floated dreamily up to the tin ceiling.

Nell groaned. "You know. It comes after Thanksgiving. A tree and presents and carols."

Ilse's eyes cleared. "Oh. Christmas. But I have to get more poems ready. I don't have time for Christmas this year. I know," her face brightened, "we can celebrate it later. Perhaps April would be a good month. April 25th, the Willows' Christmas."

The fork fell, leaving a dot of orange squash stuck to the linoleum. Ilse had lost her mind. Christmas in April?

When Tip stomped in, adding mud and snow to the squash on the floor, Nell appealed to him.

"Christmas is two weeks away, but Mom wants to put it off until April."

He put down the pail of milk and shrugged out of his coat. "This is too much. Too much for ordinary human beings. The Farm always took care of holidays. Maybe your mother is right. April would be better. Besides, I'm just getting over making that Thanksgiving dinner."

"Abigail needs Christmas," Nell said stoutly. "I'll take care of it for you. Only I need money. You know, for presents and lights and stuff. You could cut down a pine, Dad. And Mom could make cookies."

Ilse cleared her papers from the table. "Do you have any money, Tip?"

He pulled a flat wallet from his jeans. "Sixty dollars. Think that's enough?"

Nell had no idea what anything cost, but sixty dollars seemed to be enough. "That's twenty dollars apiece. You and Mom and Abigail. I won't buy anything for me. You'll have to buy my present, otherwise it won't be a surprise. If it's not a surprise, it's not a present."

Tip nodded, his lips counting out the money, but Ilse seemed lost in her papers again.

Nell put the money in her mitten and stuffed it in the pocket of her coat. She went back to the oven to take care of the squash before beginning on the milk. "I'll be shopping tomorrow, so I'll be late. Please take care of Abigail for me."

Ilse heard that. "Oh, Nell," she groaned. "Christmas is not *that* important. Hurry home."

The street lights flickered on before Nell left school the next day. She fingered the money in her mitten. The presents she bought would have to be small so she could carry them home. As she walked up Main Street, she thought about Jack. Maybe she should ask for Jack for her present. She had no idea what a dog cost, but it couldn't be more than the twenty dollars she had for each person in the family.

In the secondhand bookstore she found a book of poetry for her mother. This was easy. Inside the cover was penciled $1.00. She got a book on how to get your writing published for Tip. That was $1.50. A floppy cloth book was just right for Abigail and it was only seventy-five cents. A copy of *Little House on the Prairie* sat on the shelf, but she passed it by. She could not buy herself a present.

Across the street in a crowded store with slanting floors, she found a string of tiny lights, each light in the shape of a flower. She paid $2.98 for the string, and finished her purchases with a plush bear for Abigail that cost $4.98. That was all she could carry in one day. The woman behind the counter gave her a large shopping bag to hold the presents as well as her homework. The bag bumped against her legs as she walked and cut her fingers with its weight.

When the kitchen was spotless after dinner, Nell headed for the stairs. "I couldn't do all the shopping in one day, Mom. I'll be late again tomorrow." Nell raced up the stairs before Ilse had time to get out of the front room.

Safely shut in her room, Nell did her homework in the winking, blinking light of the string of flowers. It wasn't good for her eyes, but the lights soothed her with their promise that Christmas would come to the Willows in Maine.

———

Snow began right after morning recess. First small flakes slowly drifted from a leaden sky, then the flakes grew larger, forming a silent veil outside the window. Mrs. Cavendish turned on the overhead lights.

The lunchroom was cold and dreary. "This snow isn't going to stop," Daniel said. "Why don't you have a cup of cocoa at my house before you start home?"

The room suddenly seemed brighter. Nell had wanted to see Daniel's house since that first day of school in September.

Darkness settled in as they crossed the bridge and turned onto the wharf. Snowflakes dimpled the smooth water.

"I never thought of snow falling into the ocean. It seems like such a waste," Nell said.

"The snow will stay when the harbor starts to freeze."

They stepped from the wharf to the porch that wrapped around three sides of Daniel's house. The weathered gray shingles blended into the snow, but the door facing the ocean wore blue paint and had ships' running lights on either side, one green, one red.

"Come in, come in. I've heard so much about you, Nell." It was a warm voice with a built-in chuckle. Nell stepped into the living room that stretched the length of the house.

Daniel's mother wore a shapeless gray skirt half-covered by a soft, drooping sweater. Beneath the sleeves hung two curled-up hands, large bumps of bones pulling the skin white. Her soft shoes were slashed to make room for misshapen feet.

"Arthritis. Can you imagine someone with arthritis living right over the damp ocean?"

Nell shook her head, though she knew nothing about

arthritis. She only knew that she liked Mrs. Rhodes's large gray eyes and chuckling voice. "This is a nice room. I love those rag rugs."

"Thank you. I made them myself. I can still coax these hands to do what I want them to."

Mr. Rhodes came in the front door, shaking snow from his curling beard. "This is the place to be on a day like this."

Sipping her cocoa slowly, Nell listened to Daniel and his parents talk about their day. She pretended that this was where she lived. Beneath them, the tide slip-slapped against the pilings. When her cup was empty she glanced at the window and saw herself reflected in its blackness. Hurriedly she put on her coat and thanked the Rhodeses before running off into the darkness.

In the dry goods store Nell found warm gloves and scarves for Tip and Ilse and a knitted hat for Abigail. As she walked back to the cash register, a wooden horse on wheels caught her eye. The horse was painted white and had large, dark eyes and a red mane, tail, and saddle. It was Abigail-size.

Nell paid for everything, which left $1.89 in her mitten. The horse was packed in a cardboard box with instructions on the outside for putting it together. It wasn't heavy, but it was certainly clumsy to carry. By the time she left town and headed down the long road toward home, she wished she had not bought the horse.

The pile of presents on her closet floor filled Nell with a warm feeling. She forced her tired legs down the stairs to the kitchen. Just a few more steps, she promised her legs, but Tip surprised her by saying he was ready to cut the Christmas tree.

Wind blew the snow waist deep in parts of the field. Nell stretched complaining legs to follow in Tip's footprints. Pines were not the best trees to hang things on, as the branches were so floppy, but she found a small sturdy triangle of a tree with blobs of snow clinging to its needles. "This is the one."

Tip sawed awkwardly, but once the saw bit through the bark, it settled into a rhythm. Tip's soft voice could barely be heard over the sound of the saw.

"This tree's a lonely thing, growing at the edge of the woods. The trees farther back are safer from the wind."

The tree wobbled as the saw broke the bark on the opposite side. Nell held the trunk steady and listened to Tip.

"There are people who are alone, like this tree. They mourn parts of their bodies and dream terrible dreams. They need to know that others are going through the same terrible things."

He picked up the trunk end, and Nell held the top. Needles brushed her face, enveloping her with the smell of Christmas.

"You're not alone, Dad. You have Mom and Abigail and me."

"Everyone's alone inside himself. I'm glad I have you, Muffin."

Tip didn't talk often, and Nell felt a warm closeness, even though they walked in the cold evening air with a tree between them.

"I never went to college. It's hard for me to write with my left hand." Tip paused for breath between his words.

"But I have things I have to say. It's very important to me, Nell."

"How do you know what to write? I have trouble with my journal. By the time I put something down, the rest of it has gone away."

The tree went up and down as Tip limped ahead. "I don't know. I guess you write what's important to you. That's what I'm trying to do."

Tip had told her about the shrapnel in his head and had showed her his medal, but she had never heard the whole story. "When you finish writing it, Dad, I want to be the first to read your story."

"You will," he promised.

Tip made a stand for the tree and stood it in a corner of the kitchen. The single string of lights made several circles around the pine. Nell plugged them in before she started supper. "Light," Abigail cried, pointing to the tree. She lay down and looked upward at the blinking lights.

"That's right," Nell said. "And soon it will be Christmas, and Abigail will get some presents. Everyone will get presents," she said loudly, hoping her parents were listening.

Nell had forgotten wrapping paper and ribbon, so while her parents put Abigail to bed, she sneaked into the front room. Ilse had neat piles of writing paper in different colors, blue, green, pink, and yellow, and Nell gathered some of each. Tip kept tape on the shelf, and she took that, too. She quietly returned to her room, closed the door, and began taping the paper together. The books were easy, and by the time she got to the boxes with the gloves and scarves and the hat, she had learned how to fold the corners and tape them neatly. The stuffed bear and the horse had too many curves and angles for her to wrap stiff writing paper around them, so she left them unwrapped.

I don't know, she wrote in her journal that night. *I told them I couldn't buy myself a present. They've seen me carrying things up to my room when I come home from school. But I haven't smelled any cookies baking. Tip and Ilse have not gone to the store. But parents don't forget their daughter on Christmas, do they?* She closed her journal and tucked it under her pillow. Most parents wouldn't forget their daughter. Mimi's parents wouldn't. Daniel's parents wouldn't, either. But Tip and Ilse? She wrapped her quilt around her and curled up into a ball in her bed. An ache in her stomach warned her that the Willows had a hard time remembering things.

13

On Christmas morning Nell dressed quickly before
bringing down the presents she'd wrapped. She stacked
them around the pine and placed the white horse where
Abigail would see it first, then set the bear firmly on the
painted saddle. Then she made muffins, dotting them
with last summer's raspberry jam.

"Look, Abigail. Santa's been here and left presents
under the tree." Ilse put the baby down. Nell noticed
that Ilse carried nothing else.

Oh well, Nell thought, Ilse had to carry Abigail down,
and it was hard to carry such a wriggly little one. It was
Tip she could depend on. Tip is so kind, just like Daniel.
He wouldn't let her down.

Abigail ran to the white horse, picked up the bear,

climbed into the red saddle, and soon had the horse moving on its wheels around the kitchen, under the table, and out into the hall. Tip steered her back again. He came down fully dressed as usual, brace on, hidden by trousers and boots. His hands, like Ilse's, were empty.

Nell poured coffee into two mugs. He's just playing with me, she thought. He'll make a big show pretending to have forgotten me, and then I'll be more surprised. But her stomach hurt more than it had the other night. She sat with her arms wrapped tightly around her middle.

Tip played Santa, giving out the packages one by one. Ilse, Abigail, Tip, Abigail, Ilse, Tip . . . and then they were all gone. Sheets of colored paper littered the floor and the bare linoleum under the pine tree reflected the blinking lights.

Nell sat on the wooden chair at the kitchen table in a circle of quiet. She had believed up to this minute that Tip would snap his fingers and say he'd just remembered something, or Ilse would slip out into the front room. But Tip and Ilse still sat on the floor and watched Abigail hug her new bear.

A burning smell rose from the oven. Tip pulled himself up to rescue the muffins. "No problem. Just cut off the bottoms and they're good as new." He said this to comfort Nell, then seemed to realize that she didn't care about the muffins. He put the pan on the stove and turned off the oven before walking over to her.

He tipped up her chin with his finger. "You did a great job shopping for us." He paused on the word, "us." "And that's exactly what you said you'd do." He hit his forehead with the palm of his hand, not violently to shake something loose, but firmly as if he was trying to stuff words in. "You did your part, and we forgot ours. How could two people be so stupid!"

Nell looked into his dark eyes and saw herself reflected. She shook her own dark curls, angry at seeing herself looking so unhappy. "I never cry," she said.

"No, you never do." He was about to say something else, but they both heard Rose's bellows. Christmas or no Christmas, cows had to be milked.

Tip picked up his new gloves and scarf. "Ilse, you take care of the breakfast. I'll be in shortly."

Ilse stroked her new scarf draped around the collar of her robe, and kept her eyes on her book of poetry. "Now, what was that all about?"

Nell ran for the front hall. She might not cry, but she was angry. Furious. Feet in boots, arms in coat, she was about to go. Out.

Tip came in the front door. "Rose is all right. I'll milk her in a minute. I had a feeling you might take off." He put his hands on Nell's shoulders. "We'd fall apart without you, you know. Please be patient with us. There's just too much to do. I never know what to do first."

"Couldn't we go back to The Farm? That government money doesn't do us any good."

Tip squeezed her shoulders. "Money. Is there any of that Christmas money left?"

Nell shook her mitten. Coins jangled. "There's $1.89. I saved it for you. I couldn't buy myself a present. If it's not a surprise, it's not a present."

Tip emptied Nell's mitten into his hand. "I didn't listen, as usual. *We* didn't listen." He put the change in his pocket, then pulled a twenty-dollar bill from his wallet. "This is a surprise. That makes it a real present. Spend it all on yourself. *That* is an order."

Nell folded the bill and put it in her mitten. She hadn't torn the wrapping paper off, or shaken it to guess what it was, but it was a surprise, and by her rules that made it a present. Then why did a present make her feel like crying?

14

Dark store windows lined Blue Harbor's silent Main Street. Unread signs on doors said politely, SORRY, WE'RE CLOSED. Nell crackled the bill inside her mitten. What could she buy that would make up for a lost Christmas? She crossed the bridge slowly and caught a glimpse of twinkling lights in Daniel's window. They were probably eating breakfast. Nell's stomach growled, reminding her of the raspberry muffins she had not touched.

The wind flattened the marsh grass as she walked past the school and turned down Mimi's street. She definitely needed a scarf like the ones she'd bought for Tip and Ilse.

When she ran out of the house, Nell had taken her familiar school route out of habit. Now she wondered where she was going. Could she drop in at Mimi's house this early in the morning? Mr. Tompkins came out of the barn and hailed her.

"No one walks the streets on Christmas Day," he said. "Come join us for breakfast."

Breakfast sounded wonderful, and the thought of seeing her Jack was even more wonderful. Nell followed Mr. Tompkins through the back door and was greeted by a warm cloud of cinnamon and sage. Inside, small trucks zoomed across the floor, bumping into empty boxes, crumpled paper, and ribbon.

Mimi leaped over two kneeling children to grab Nell's hand. "Come, see what I got." She led Nell to her pile of presents—a red corduroy shirt, a pair of knee socks, a box of pastels, and a sketchbook. "The kids gave me these." She lifted a necklace of clay beads, a one-legged gingerbread man, and a scrapbook. "What did you get?"

"I came to wish Jack a merry Christmas," Nell said quickly. "Dad said I could buy anything I wanted. I want my own dog."

They huddled over the box and watched Jack climb over the other puppies to push his wet nose against Nell's hand.

"Save your money for dog food," Mimi said. "He's going to be a big eater."

Nell held the wriggling puppy and kissed its soft neck. "When can I take him?"

"Any time after a week or so. I'll even start paper-training him." Mimi stood up. "I'm hungry. The kids got us up at four this morning. Come on."

There was fresh milk and hot tea, homemade bread with plump raisins, and a small crock of homemade butter. No one asked why Nell spent Christmas morning with them, they just passed the food around until Nell was warm, inside and out.

"Let's do something special tomorrow," Mimi said later as she walked with Nell down the snow-covered street.

"Meet me at the bookstore at ten. I've got some money to spend." Nell watched as Mimi swooped back to her warm, crowded house. Now that there was something to look forward to, it wasn't as hard to go home.

Ilse didn't say a word about Nell's missing presents or her absence for the whole morning, but she cooked dinner and refused help with the dishes. Nell decided this was Ilse's way of saying she was sorry.

Tip sat at the table, reading his new book. Abigail sleepily rode her white horse down the hall and back. When Ilse reached for her book of poetry, Nell decided it was now or never. She cleared her throat.

"Tomorrow I'm going Christmas shopping. For me." She spoke faster. "Mimi gave me a puppy. He can come in a week or so. His name is Jack." She ran upstairs before anyone could argue with her.

Nell read the last entry in her journal. What would Mrs. Cavendish think when she read Nell's fears that her parents would forget her at Christmas? She was betraying her own parents. If only her diary was truly secret, she could admit they had forgotten her.

I got twenty whole dollars to spend all on myself, she wrote. *I am going to get Jack, when he's ready to leave his mother.* Those were not lies. She put her pencil down, but continued to write in her head. *They did forget me.*

I knew they would. I wish I knew how to make them love me.

"It's so good to be out of the house." Mimi inhaled the fishy smells of the harbor. "When I grow up I'm going to live in an empty room with just a bed."

"I had a room like that on The Farm. All I did there was sleep. When I grow up I'm going to have loads of kids and hug them all day long." Nell nibbled on a necklace of colored candies on a string. Mimi's necklace hung around her coat collar. Nell wore a new rose-pink hat and matching scarf, and carried a secondhand copy of *Little House on the Prairie*. A small dog collar was fastened around her wrist, and her pink mitten jingled with change.

Small boats chugged out of the harbor. Cars were parked along the street and even on the bridge. "Wonder what's up," Mimi said. "After Christmas the harbor's usually quiet."

"Bo-at's late coming in," a fisherman said, his face creased with worry.

Nell looked up in alarm. Someone in a blue parka stood on Daniel's porch. She raced across the dock with Mimi at her heels.

"Pop went out to bring in the last of his traps. That was about seven, and now it's almost two. Ma just called the Coast Guard." Daniel talked to Nell and Mimi, but he never took his eyes from the harbor.

Nell stood next to Daniel; Mimi on his other side. His arms shook, a little flutter against Nell's coat sleeve. She wanted to comfort him, but there was no sign of the boat, and empty words would not help. She tried to think how she would feel if Tip were out there, but it was too terrible to imagine.

Mimi said, "I'm sure everything is all right, and your father will be home soon."

Mimi believed that, Nell knew. Everything always worked out for Mimi. But things did not often work out for Nell, and she knew every bit of comfort would be false.

"Your mother—is she alone?" Nell asked.

Daniel nodded.

"Think it would be all right if I went in?"

Daniel nodded again.

Nell gave a timid knock, then opened the door, hoping to save Mrs. Rhodes a shuffling trip to let her in.

Mrs. Rhodes sat at the table, as far as one could get from the ocean in that house. Nell took off her mitten and covered the misshapen hand with her own. Mrs. Rhodes pointed to a chair and Nell sat in it, still without talking.

Daniel and Mimi came in to warm their hands. "It's been too long," Daniel said.

His mother stood and put her arms around him. "My bones say everything is all right. I'll make you a sandwich. One for Pop, too. He hasn't had a thing since this morning."

Nell twisted idle hands in her lap. Tip was safer writing in the front room than collecting traps out on a boat. At least she knew where he was.

The clock ticked, the wind picked up, cars pulled away from the bridge and others took their places. Daniel's mother rattled plates in the kitchen, opening and closing the refrigerator door several times. Daniel shrugged out of his jacket, and when the hood slid off, his hair stood up as if he'd put his finger in a light socket. His eyes were pink and filmy with tears about to spill. Nell had never seen Tip cry, and looked down at her hands rather than see Daniel's tears.

The mournful sound of the fire siren broke the silence. "Something's happening," Nell said.

Mimi pushed her bangs straight up, giving her face a defenseless look. "It could be a fire somewhere."

Daniel flew to the window overlooking the ocean. "They're towing his boat in. I don't see him."

Forgetting coats, the four went out on the porch. Mrs. Rhodes moved faster than anyone. Sirens and whistles sounded as a parade of boats moved into the harbor. Daniel jumped down to the dock and stood, one foot on a cleat, ready to leap into the freezing water if necessary.

The lead boat towed the lobster boat to the dock, where several men lifted a blanket-wrapped figure to shore.

Daniel bent over his father, then raised his fingers in a sign of victory. Nell sagged against the railing, warm relief flooding over her. Mrs. Rhodes went to the stairs, clasping and unclasping her knotted hands as she watched the rescuers carry her husband up to the porch.

"He's all right," Daniel whispered as the men put his father into the bedroom. "Engine conked out. He drifted to the far side of one of those little islands."

"Why did they carry him off the boat, then?" Mimi asked.

"He got too cold. He's been out there a while. Doc's on his way."

Nell and Mimi gathered their things and slipped out, leaving Daniel and his mother with their arms around each other.

"Whew," Mimi said, turning in circles on the dock. "Too much excitement for me. I'm going home to read."

"Me, too," Nell said, waving her new book.

The wind played with the ends of Nell's muffler as she walked the bleak road home. At least she knew where Tip was. Daniel hadn't known where his father was for most of the day. Whatever she wanted Tip to be, it was not a lobsterman.

15

School resumed the day after New Year's. Nell stirred long before dawn, eager to escape. After her shopping trip, the vacation had turned into one long baby-sitting and cooking job while Tip and Ilse worked on their writing.

There was no telling what kind of day it would be, for the sky was still black with two stars hanging on the horizon. The sky had lightened when Nell got to town, but it was still too early for school. She hesitated a moment before stepping onto Daniel's porch.

Daniel opened the door, but it was his mother's warm voice that welcomed her. "Come in, child. Cocoa? Daniel, please get another cup."

Nell stepped in and saw Mr. Rhodes sitting at the table. "Are you all right?"

His face creased into a thousand wrinkles. "I was worried about my feet, but they're fine. I'm thinking of fishing, now that all my traps are in."

"You're mighty early," Daniel said. "What's up?"

"Now, don't go prying." Daniel's mother poured the cocoa. "You *are* all right, aren't you?" She peered at Nell in a motherly way.

Nell burned her tongue. Was she all right? "Sure. I just love school, that's all."

"That means she's not all right," Daniel teased. "She's crazy."

"Is your father farming that little piece of land?" Mr. Rhodes asked.

"Some. But mostly he's writing."

Mrs. Rhodes set a piece of toast in front of Nell. "Your mother writes, too, doesn't she? My, what a clever family. There's quite a colony of writers and artists here in the summer. They have parties at the art gallery."

Nell brightened. "We had a party in the fall. Sometimes my mother gets very sad. A party would cheer her up."

As they crossed the bridge, Nell said to Daniel, "I think it would take more than a party to cheer my mother. I think she needs . . . Oh, I don't know what she needs. She just needs."

Mrs. Cavendish hopped around the room like a mother bird feeding her young. "We're going to study poetry the next few weeks," she chirped. "Mr. Quimby will choose the best poems, and we'll print them in a class newspaper."

Poetry. She couldn't seem to get away from it. Nell

made a face at Mimi, who crossed her eyes in agreement.

At recess the two girls sat on a rock at the edge of the playing field and worked on their poems.

"Writing poetry is like doing a puzzle," Mimi said, moving her pencil with mittened fingers.

"Sort of habit forming," Nell agreed. "I can see why Ilse got hooked. I don't think poetry is good for you."

"Why do you always call your mother by her first name?" Mimi asked. "In our family, it's not allowed."

"Sometimes I call her Mom. We all used first names on The Farm, where we were one big family. Too many Moms and Dads could be confusing. Besides, I think it suits Ilse. Your mother is a real mother, but Ilse isn't." After she'd said that, Nell felt she had been unkind. Ilse just needed more practice, and then she'd be a real mother.

The house was cold. The furnace didn't run fast enough to warm the January air seeping in around the edges of doors and windows. Ilse sat at the kitchen table, her gloved fingers stuffing papers into a manila envelope. Abigail slept beside her in her chair hooked to the table, sticky face resting on sticky arms.

"Your father got a call from Boston. There's someone interested in what he's writing. I'm going to run him in to catch the 5:15 bus. Go out and hurry him up. He's milking when he should be getting ready."

Frigid air slapped Nell's face. The shed didn't look any different than it had on the day of the barbecue, except that Nell had added a few more boards wherever she could reach. Rose would freeze if the weather got much colder.

Tip looked up, his dark eyes flashing. "An editor likes my work." He spoke softly, as always, but his voice sounded like a shout of joy.

She knelt beside him. "If you're going to Boston, you'd better give me a milking lesson. A bulldozer couldn't push Ilse out here."

Tip guided her hands until milk foamed into the pail. "Speak softly, and be gentle. Rose is a good girl. She knows we like her." He took his hands away, and Nell kept up the same rhythm. "Actually, it's great exercise. Even my bad hand does some of the work."

"You ought to put that in your book, Dad." Maybe her wish that Tip should go off to work like other fathers was not right for him. "Don't you think it's too cold for Rose out here?"

"I know, I know. I put off fixing this shed for too long. I'll only be gone a day or two. I promise I'll finish it when I get back. It's up to you to keep things going. Be sure your mother shops for food and orders a load of hay."

When Nell carried the pail of milk into the kitchen, the truck was gone. She started dinner, thinking that Tip's good-bye could have included a kiss along with the list of things to do.

Ilse came in carrying Abigail in one arm and the mail in the other. "So much excitement today I forgot to bring in the mail." She handed Abigail to Nell and opened a long, creamy-colored envelope.

"Look, look what Professor Stephenson wrote. He sent my poems to a publishing house in New York." Ilse's fingers shook as she dangled the letter in front of Nell.

Nell read the words slowly. "They want you to come

to New York to talk about putting your poems in a book. That's great."

Nell took Abigail's snowsuit off before serving her dinner. "Dad'll be home soon, probably the day after tomorrow. Then, I guess, you'll be going. He said to tell you to get food and hay."

Ilse folded the letter and slipped it back into the envelope. "Oh, you can't know how much this means to me. How did I ever get so sidetracked? All those years wasted."

Ilse's face was pink, her eyes shining. She didn't seem to know she was standing in a small kitchen in a little house in Maine. Those wasted years? Did she mean the ones she had spent with Tip and with Abigail and Nell?

Hands behind her back, Ilse strode around the room making plans in a businesslike way. "After dinner we'll make out a shopping list. Tomorrow I'll buy the groceries. Then I'll take a bus to the city."

"No. You can't leave us. I have to go to school. It's the law."

Ilse brushed lawbreaking aside the way she brushed hair back from her eyes. "It can't be for more than a day. The minute Tip gets home you can go to school again. For heaven's sake, what's a few days if it means a book for me?"

A day's vacation didn't sound too bad to Nell. She could reread her book, work on her poem, and teach Abigail a few more words. But then she thought of Daniel waiting on the dock for her in the morning, and Mimi sitting next to an empty desk, and the day off didn't seem all that great.

———

The next morning went quickly. As planned, Ilse went out early and brought home groceries and hay. She tipped the bales of hay off the truck for Nell to roll to the shed, then carried the food inside. While Ilse stocked the pantry, Nell went out to move the hay.

The cold took Nell's breath away, and she missed Tip's warm hands on hers when she milked Rose.

Ilse also took Nell's breath away when she appeared downstairs in a suit, her hair twisted up in a shining knot.

"I know you girls will be just fine." Ilse picked up a large envelope full of papers along with the old suitcase. The last time Nell had seen that suitcase was when they left The Farm. "If your father calls, tell him I left the truck behind the IGA. Be good."

The house settled into quiet after the slamming of the door. Nell's shoulders ached, probably from moving the bales of hay. The clock in the kitchen stood at social studies time, but Abigail's yawn said it was time to take a nap.

I don't mind being alone, Nell told herself. But this was not like being alone watching the lambs or walking to school. Never in her whole life had both Tip and Ilse been away at the same time.

Nell felt closer to her parents in the front room, where she looked at Ilse's empty desktop and touched the pile of returned manuscripts on Tip's table. Maybe there was a book she could read that would fill the time. She ran her eyes over the shelves and picked out a tall, narrow book with the word KENTON on the binding. When she opened it, she discovered it was Ilse's college yearbook.

Graff, Ilse, she read. The picture was of a younger Ilse, pale blond hair curling on her shoulders, serious face looking off into the distance. She looked like a movie star. Ilse had been on the debating team, edited the literary magazine, had been a member of the school orchestra, and top scholar in her class her last three years. Nell was not surprised at all by the list of honors that went to someone who only got A's. She once was a guest editor of a New York magazine, was granted a scholarship to study for a summer in an Ivy League college, and won a full scholarship for her senior year.

In the back of the book Nell found another picture of Ilse in a dark sweater and plaid skirt, holding a flute. Nell had never known her mother played the flute. Messages were written over many of the pictures. *I know you will succeed. Best of luck with your writing.* It was like meeting her mother for the first time.

Nell searched the shelves for something of Tip's. At last she found it, a yearbook from Charlestown High School. *Willow, Thomas.* No mention of the Ian or Philip. He looked angry in his picture. All that was mentioned under activities was that he'd played freshman football. This was not her gentle, loving Tip, but a rough young stranger who looked ready for a fight.

Nell was puzzled. How had two totally different people gotten together? She closed the books and slipped them back on the shelf.

She tuned the radio to the public station. A woman was talking about cooking. Cooking was a wonderful idea. Nell made spice cookies and soon had the kitchen smelling as good as Mimi's. If Jack were lying in the corner, she might feel almost happy.

Abigail woke, warm and fretful. Nell gave her a cookie and set her on the little white horse. "Cookie," Nell said.

"Cookie," Abigail said clearly. She crammed the whole thing in her mouth and demanded, "Gookie," less clearly.

"Finish that one first," Nell said.

Abigail rode in a circle, chewing furiously. She stopped in front of Nell, opened her mouth to show it was empty, then put out her hand. "Cookie, pease."

Nell laughed. "Okay, charmer, but this is the last one. You've got to save room for supper."

Taking the second cookie, Abigail rode her horse under the table and down the hall to the front door, leaving a trail of crumbs behind her. She came back and pulled at Nell's jeans. "Cookie, pease," she said, lifting her head and smiling, showing baby teeth.

"You can't charm me into a third cookie. I'll give you one after supper," Nell said matter-of-factly.

Then Abigail did something Nell had never seen her do before. She dropped from her horse to the floor, curling in a crouched position so her head touched her knees, and let out a long scream.

Nell tried to pick her up, but she was rigid with anger and stayed in the same crouch when Nell lifted her off the floor. Gone was the happy, relaxed little girl Nell had watched the summer before. In her place was a ball of fury. Nell put her back on the floor.

"Cook, cook, cook," Abigail sobbed, only stopping to breathe once in a while before continuing the same cry.

No wonder Ilse was so quick to leave, Nell thought. How could an angel at one year turn into a monster at almost two? Suddenly Nell felt out of control. Should she give in and hand her sister a cookie? Would it be safe to let her cry for long? Not knowing the answers, she left Abigail sobbing on the floor and went into the front room and put *The 1812 Overture* on the stereo. She turned the volume up until she could feel the vibrations through the floor. If Abigail had to cry, at least it would be harder to hear her.

The sobs turned to sniffling and hiccupping, and Abigail's red face subsided to pink. She made one last try with a plaintive, "Orsie wants cookie," and getting no response, got up and mounted the horse again. Nell gave a long sigh. The storm had passed.

Nell's next worry was what would she do with her sister when it was time to milk Rose? Before darkness fell she dragged heavy chairs from the front room and, laying them down on the floor, made a cage. She put Abigail inside with her favorite measuring cups.

"Be good," Nell whispered, the same words Ilse had said when she left.

Rose was slow letting down her milk. The frigid pine woods crackled and popped with the suddenness of rifle shots. Rose's milk filled only half the pail, and she switched her tail irritably as if to say, that's all there is. Nell threw her another flake of hay and latched the door on the way out to keep the wind from banging it against the wall.

The radio played all evening, low enough for Nell to hear the phone ring when Tip called. She worked on her poem, changing words here and there. Abigail whimpered. No sense putting her upstairs in her crib where she would be alone. Nell dragged the crib mattress down and set it inside the barricade of chairs.

Later she brought her own quilt and pillow down so

she could lie next to Abigail, who slept happily in her little prison. The eleven o'clock weather report warned that a storm threatened the coast. Nell felt a stab of fear, thinking of Rose in her poor excuse of a shed, of Tip limping somewhere on snowy Boston Streets, and of Ilse lost in the canyons of New York City.

16

The blizzard hit at three in the morning, howling around the wooden kitchen door, pinging snow crystals against the windows. Abigail breathed softly, but Nell sat up, wide awake. The wind made more noise than anything she'd ever heard on The Farm. Doors rattled. Any minute she expected the wind to rush into the room, slamming the door back against the wall. A crack, a groan, a thud outside, set her imagination wild. Staring into the darkness, Nell imagined Rose's shed flying apart, board by board, or the apple tree crashing to the ground. Gusts of frigid air whipped under the back door and played around the makeshift beds on the floor. She pictured Tip falling and being buried in huge drifts of snow. Only Ilse remained safe, riding in a carriage like the Snow Queen, little boys hitching rides behind her.

The house shook with the onslaught of wind till Nell could stand it no longer. She turned on the overhead light, which bounced against the tin ceiling and glanced off the black windows. The bending shapes of trees cast eerie shadows. Nell made a cup of tea, then wrapped herself in her quilt and sat at the table. She could put on some music to cover the sounds of the wind, but she didn't dare walk down the dark hall to the front room. Besides, if Abigail woke, there might be another storm.

Sitting there listening to the wind, she tried to form some plan for escape. Maybe she should get their coats and boots, but if her parents' bedroom began to fall in on them there wouldn't be time to dress and still get out the door. If the door blew in, she would carry Abigail into the front room and hide under the desk. She pulled the quilt tightly around her. After many months of handling things, learning how to cook and to take care of the house and Abigail, all of a sudden there was nothing she could do. She was responsible for the house and for Abigail, but the wind had taken charge.

"Oh, Tip, where are you?" Hot tears fell into the cooling tea.

The wind died down long after her cup was cold, and the kitchen seemed brighter. Nell got up and turned on the radio, which surprised her by giving the seven o'clock news. She had expected the new day to desert her the way Tip and Ilse had. The newscaster announced that record cold made plowing difficult and residents were advised to stay home. All schools in Blue Harbor would be closed. Good. She might miss only one day of school.

"Oh, what a goose am I," she said aloud. Her tears had not been necessary. Tip and Ilse would be home soon, Abigail had slept through the whole storm, and the house still stood, warm and safe.

The wind burned her face, and her feet turned to lumps of ice, as Nell struggled past Ilse's snow-covered garden to Rose's shed. She shifted the pail of water from one frozen hand to the other as she looked around the yard. Neat piles of snow covered the odds and ends of last summer's herbs and the untidy squares of roof shingles still lying by the shed. Nell realized why the kitchen was so dark. A wall of snow on one side of the house reached from the ground to the eaves, covering the windows. At least the snow would keep the house warmer.

Rose tossed her head from side to side, a wild look in her bulging eyes, as Nell tried to milk her. Snow covered the cracks in the back of the shed, keeping the wind out, but the amount of milk in the pail was less than it had been the night before. "I wish I could take you in the house with us," Nell whispered into Rose's velvety ear.

During the first full day of Ilse's absence, Abigail played happily, riding her white horse, stopping to shape balls of dough. Nell kept the kitchen warm with bread in the oven and a pot of soup simmering on the back burner. As she cooked, she sang "Twinkle, Twinkle" over and over. There were no more tantrums, and whatever had fallen with a thud in the night had not damaged anything. Nell relaxed a bit. When Tip came home, she would sleep for a week.

Night closed down before four. Nell set Abigail into the chair barricade, then she dressed in a double layer of clothes. Her boots squeaked and water slopped from the pail, making holes in the snow as she struggled to the shed.

Rose stared straight ahead as if tired of tail-switching and head-shaking, letting down only enough milk to cover the bottom of the pail. Nell was glad. She wanted to get back into the house, afraid Tip or Ilse might call while she was outside.

The telephone did not ring. Sometime in the night the oil burner thunked and stopped its rumbling. The silence was more frightening than the wind of the night before. Once again Nell sat at the table, wishing the night away.

The next morning, she went down to the cellar, closing the door solidly behind her so Abigail wouldn't fall down the stairs. She hurried across the dirt floor and kicked the oil tank. It echoed hollowly. Empty.

Where were they? Parents were supposed to be home. Nell mixed the last of the milk with cereal and gave it to Abigail, while she pondered the trouble they were in. If there was no heat, soon the pipes would burst and there would be no water. She still had Rose to feed and milk, and the phone to answer.

While Abigail made designs with her cereal, Nell ran the water in the kitchen and bathroom, hoping the trickle would keep the pipes from freezing. The window not covered with snow seemed to have grown thicker, like heavy glass brick, making it impossible to see outside.

Finally, Abigail was once again in her chair cage and Nell braved the trip to the shed. Cold, thin rain made the snow slick. Nell blinked rapidly to keep her wet eyelashes from sticking together as she slipped and slid, dragging the pail along the frozen surface.

Still air chilled her bones as she opened the shed door.

Nell tripped on something hard in the straw and fell against the splintery wall, the pail taking a sharp bite of her shin. She ran her hand down her leg. It was just water, not blood. Gradually her eyes adjusted to the dimness of the snow-covered shed. She focused on the walls, then at the patched roof, but kept from looking down to see what had tripped her. She had known from the minute she stepped into that cold, dead air. Rose lay on her side, her front legs stiff and straight out, her rear legs slightly parted by her frozen udder.

Nell backed out of the shed, still holding the pail with whatever water was left, and carried the pail back across the ice and into the kitchen where she set it on the drain board as carefully as if it held freshly laid eggs. She wanted to give an Abigail-scream and tuck her head between her knees, but that wouldn't help anyone. Not poor, dead Rose, not Abigail, and not herself. She had to keep the scream inside until Tip came. Dear, dear Tip. How sad he would be when he found out about Rose. Nell was powerless as the tears started. She had never seen anything dead before, not even the animals that were slaughtered at The Farm. Poor, poor Rose; warm, lovely Rose, so cold and stiff.

Abigail pulled herself up in the chair cage and smiled broadly, as if amused by her sister's tears. "Da da, da da, da da da," Abigail sang happily to the tune of "Twinkle, Twinkle, Little Star."

17

Nell moved briskly around the kitchen. Water still ran from the faucet, there was still gas and electricity, and the pantry was full. Missing were milk, heat, and Ilse and Tip. She lighted the oven to keep the kitchen warm. If only the phone would ring. Neither Tip nor Ilse had left a number for her to call. Nell was sure that Tip thought Ilse was home taking care of things, and that Ilse was just as certain Tip had returned from Boston.

Nell got down the calendar and checked off the dates. Tip had left on the second of January, and Ilse on the third. Yesterday had been the fourth, the first full day they were both gone. It was also the day after the blizzard, so they probably were snowed in somewhere.

The horror of finding Rose dead ate at Nell's insides.

For a girl who never cried, she was doing more than her share. She should have brought Rose in and closed her in the front room. It would have served Tip and Ilse right if their precious papers had ended up in one of Rose's four stomachs.

Abigail whimpered, then pulled herself up on a chair. Nell gave one last, sobbing sigh. At least Abigail would take her mind off Rose. She picked up the baby and hugged her tight.

"We'll be fine, little one," she whispered into the baby's soft neck. She changed and dressed Abigail on the kitchen table, then turned off the oven and set her on the floor.

The world outside was a dark and slippery place. It was not a place to take a baby. If Nell called the Rhodeses or the Tompkinses, they would ask where her parents were. Saying they had left her and Abigail would be like tattling, and Nell refused to do that.

What would Laura have done? If Ma and Pa Ingalls had not been able to get home, Laura would have kept the fire going and taken care of baby Carrie.

"Cookie, pease," Abigail said.

Nell was in no mood for another tantrum, and handed the little a girl a cookie.

"Oh, scissors! Where are Tip and Ilse?" Miz Moore had taught the children that words beginning with "S" made good swear words. "Ring, slam it, ring," she commanded the phone hanging silent in the hall.

Later, in the afternoon, while Abigail napped, Nell started a stew. The radio announcer said the roads were clear and schools would be in session the next day. During the night the temperature would dip below zero.

While Abigail was safely in her cage, Nell turned on the oven and ran water into all the empty pots in case the pipes froze.

Mimi was probably playing with the puppies. As soon as Tip or Ilse called, Nell would find out how Jack was doing. The phone filled her thoughts. Maybe the lines were down. She went into the hall and lifted the receiver. A pleasant hum warmed her ear. She hung up quickly.

Abigail woke, cranky and warm. Too warm. Nell shut off the oven to save gas for the colder night, and she dished up the stew. It tasted good, hot, and filling, but Abigail allowed only a few spoonfuls into her mouth before turning fretful again, pulling at her ears and twisting her head away. She set her mouth in a tight line and said, "Um, um," every time the spoon came near. Nell gave up. She'd do anything to avoid another of Abigail's screaming fits.

"Don't get sick," Nell said. "Please don't get sick." She found a can of apple juice and poured it into the baby's cup, feeling relieved when Abigail took a few sips. Her face was still warm, though, and her eyes had a too-bright look. Nell didn't know what to do to bring down a fever. She wiped Abigail's face with a damp cloth to cool it.

The baby sat at the table while Nell dashed upstairs to gather warm sleepers and extra blankets. She flew down before the phone could ring.

But the phone didn't ring. Abigail snuggled in her mountain of blankets and whimpered herself to sleep, but when Nell lay down and closed her eyes she saw Rose lying dead on the shed floor, soft, trusting eyes glazed over, delicate legs sticking stiffly on the straw.

Rose had been a sturdy animal with a thick hide and hair on top of that, but the weather had been too much. Nell could not keep her from dying.

Abigail had baby skin and soft, blond hair. Her only protection was what Nell gave her, a warm sleeper and blankets. She was not sturdy like Rose, and the kitchen was beginning to feel as cold as the shed. Nell didn't dare close her eyes again, fearing what she might see.

She jumped up and switched on the light over the sink. Shadows danced on the tin ceiling while she checked on Abigail, who snorted and snuffled in her sleep. She decided on a cup of tea to help her stay awake through the night. Sleepily she carried the kettle to the sink, but no water trickled from the faucet, even when she opened it as wide as it could go. With shaking hands, she poured water from one of the pans she had filled and set the kettle on a burner.

No heat, no water, no milk, no Rose. Nell walked around the kitchen trying to bring blood into her cold feet, wringing her hands partly to keep them warm and partly because she didn't know what to do with them.

When the water boiled, she made a cup of tea then wrapped herself in her quilt, tucking it under her feet and holding it tight around her neck.

Abigail coughed, a croupy sound that echoed against the tin ceiling. Had Rose coughed that last night? Nell put another blanket on her sister. Even if Rose hadn't coughed, she had died. "You can't die on me, little one," she said out loud. Abigail coughed again, then turned over. Nell waited for the next raspy breath before returning to her quilt.

"We can't stay here any longer," she said aloud. "I've

got to take Abigail to a safe place." She sipped the cooling tea slowly, hoping it would last the long, unfriendly night.

It was hard to tell when morning began, especially with the light on, but when Nell could see the telephone in the hall, she judged that other people were up and about. In the telephone book hanging from a hook in the wall, Nell found the penciled number of The Farm and dialed it before she gave herself time to think.

A woman answered, Mary, one of the kitchen women who rose early to start the stoves and put the coffee on. "This is Nell Willow," she said when the woman answered. "Tell Miz Moore to call me." She gave the number and hung up.

Nell felt a combination of relief and guilt. She had betrayed her parents, but she had to save Abigail from getting sick or freezing to death like Rose. She dragged herself back to the kitchen. Checking the calendar, she found it was the sixth of January. Tip was long overdue. He would feel so bad when he found out about Rose.

Abigail pulled herself up in her cage, her wet hair sticking to her head. That meant the fever was gone, but in this cold air, wet hair could not be good for her. Nell picked her up and rubbed her head dry with a dish towel. Then she changed her, dressing her in warm clothes and snowsuit. Neither of them had bathed for several days, but the kitchen was too cold for a bath, and there was no water, hot or cold, anyway.

Nell put a very quiet Abigail in her seat at the table and then filled the kettle with the water left in the pan. There was no milk for cocoa, but maybe she could make it with hot water. Water seemed very important now that the faucet was dry. The only thing dripping in the house was Abigail's nose. Nell slammed the kettle on the stove. She was getting very tired of this kitchen.

She had just given Abigail a piece of bread when the phone rang. Hearing Emma's voice was like a January thaw, and Nell made several tries before she found her voice. She hadn't planned what she was going to say but managed to convey in a rush of words that her parents were stuck in the storm, and there was no heat in the house, and Abigail might be getting sick.

Emma didn't hesitate. "Pack your clothes, dear. Try to keep warm. The road through the mountains is closed, so we'll have to go the long way. We'll be there by midafternoon."

Home. Nell couldn't wait to go home.

The hot cocoa perked her up. When it cooled, she gave a small cup to the baby. Abigail had shredded her bread and dropped it on the floor, and the cup joined the bread there. It was going to be a long morning. Nell mopped up, wiped Abigail's nose, and set her on her horse. She found a piece of paper and wrote a short note which she hung over the calendar with its crossed-out dates. *We've gone back to The Farm. Love, Nell.* In case Tip came home first, she added, *The truck is behind the IGA.*

Finally it was nap time, giving Nell a chance to collect their clothes. She filled two trash bags, one with dirty clothes, the other with clean clothes. She placed them by the front door, adding her quilt and a blanket, scarf, hat, and mittens. The front of the house was so cold, she put on her coat.

Now there was nothing to do but wait. Abigail ate a little soup for lunch, then Nell used the last of the precious water to wash the dishes. Ilse and Tip would be upset enough to find the girls missing. It would only make things worse to leave the house a mess.

The radio helped to keep the house alive, but waiting was not Nell's favorite pastime. She threw the rest of the stew out the kitchen door, cleaned out the refrigerator, then went upstairs and brought down her journal.

Our life in Maine is over, she wrote. *Emma and Jim are coming to take us back to The Farm.* She hesitated, then realized Mrs. Cavendish probably would never see her entry. *I don't know where Tip and Ilse are, and I'm afraid. I don't want to go back, but Rose died. It is so cold. I can't let Abigail die, too. There's nothing else I can do.*

A sharp knock at the front door set Abigail crying. Emma burst in, her full black coat flying at her sides like the wings of a bat.

"You poor lambs," Emma said, wrapping the wings around Nell. "Let me wrap the little one in that blanket and you bundle up good. We can talk in the van. Jim's out back, checking on your cow."

Nell bit her lip. "She's out there, but she doesn't need anything."

"Because she's dead," Jim said, coming in the back door. "We should have tied Tip and Ilse up and kept them with us. They can't handle the outside world any more than this baby can." He lifted Abigail, but held her at arm's length when he saw her runny nose.

Emma checked the stove to make certain it was turned off, turned off the faucets, then waved them all outside.

Soon they were in the van, the clothes in the way-back, Emma sitting next to Nell, and Abigail in a car seat they'd brought with them.

"Now, tell all," Emma said when the van started to move. The roaring engine and the rattles of the old van echoed from the metal walls and roof while Nell tried to think. How could she tell them anything and not make Tip and Ilse sound terrible?

"It was just a mix-up. I wouldn't have called you, but I thought Abigail was sick."

Jim snorted as he shifted into high gear. "Some mix-up. A dead cow. An empty oil tank. Frozen water pipes. And two children left alone in a cold house."

"Shhh, Jim," Emma warned. "The baby's gone to sleep."

Nell thought maybe Emma was keeping him from saying something bad about Tip and Ilse. She didn't care if he did. Slumping down she put her head against the cold window and fell asleep, too.

Long after dark they drove down the snow-covered road leading to The Farm. The Moores' cabin was identical to the one the Willows had lived in, and someone had set up a cot and a crib in the front room.

Nell closed her eyes and breathed in the familiar smell of the fresh, crisp Vermont air, so different from the fishy tang of Blue Harbor. She pretended she was in her old cabin with Tip and Ilse sleeping in the next room. When pictures of Rose, or of Tip frozen in a snowbank, threatened to take over, she imagined Jack curled up at her side, and, holding an imaginary Jack, she fell asleep.

18

Nell roused before the wake-up bell and listened to Abigail's snuffly breathing and the occasional creaks of mattresses as sleepers turned over in the other rooms. Uncomfortable thoughts swirled in her head. She tried concentrating on relaxing her legs and slipping back into sleep, but the thoughts were too persistent. Had Abigail been in so much danger that they had to move back to The Farm? Couldn't she have held on a little longer? Tip and Ilse must surely be back at the farmhouse by now, wondering why she couldn't have handled things, and why Rose lay dead in the shed.

Nell rolled on her side and tried to remember which leg should be drawn up, and which stretched out, but she couldn't get comfortable. If Tip and Ilse were not at home, they were probably hurt in the storm. That scared her, but not as much as another idea.

She drew both legs up, but that made her knees rub together. There could have been another reason Tip and Ilse had not come back. They didn't love her anymore. She thought of Ilse's wasted years, and knew she and Abigail were the cause. A hard knot in her throat kept her from swallowing. She tried to picture Tip's kind, dark eyes, but all she saw was his eager face as he left for the bus.

Parents did not go away and leave their children if they still loved them. Nell curled into a tight ball and held on to her legs until the morning bell awakened the others.

By the time the breakfast bell clanged, Nell had almost forgotten her early morning fears in the scramble to dress Abigail and herself, as well as to take turns in the single bathroom. Nell and Bobby set off across the snow with Abigail in between them. Emma and Jim followed more slowly, relaxing after the difficulties of sheltering two extra people in their small cabin.

Nell had forgotten Abigail's little seat that attached to the table, so she dragged a high chair across the dining hall and placed it next to Emma. Nell sat beside Bobby.

Bobby had grown a little fatter, more like his mother. Nell supposed she had changed, too, after nearly a year of doing grown-up work. "How is it on the outside?" Bobby whispered, his eyes shining with curiosity.

"It's harder," Nell said. "There's no one to help you. Sometimes there's more work than you can do."

She felt homesick when Emma walked Abigail over to the Wee Ones' corner. The baby's nose still ran, and her cheeks were chapped and red, but otherwise she seemed all right. Abigail sat right down with the other children, and Nell heard her sing "Twinkle, Twinkle." Babies were like rubber balls: the harder they were pushed, the higher they bounced.

Gradually the dining hall emptied. The adults left to do their jobs, whatever they were in this subzero weather. Nell knew there were animals to feed and cows to be milked. The whine of a chain saw reminded her that wood for next year was cut in the deep of winter.

The Big Ones gathered at their table and Nell was once again one of them. How she had longed to sit with the group last spring. Chrissie spoke shyly. "SOS. Same Old Stuff. I bet you learned plenty in a real school."

"Ay-uh," Nell said, imitating Mr. Rhodes's Maine accent. "I had seven books in my desk, and I could take them home at night. There was a library in the school. Swings and seesaws and basketball hoops on the playground. So many kids I couldn't count them. There was a cafeteria, too."

"Just for kids?" Bobby asked. It seemed harder for him to imagine eating without his family than it was to think of a library or a playground.

Emma carried a load of books and papers. "Seems like old times, having Nell here." She tore sheets of lined yellow paper from a large pad, passing out one sheet to each student. "Listen carefully while I read the problems."

Nell looked over at Bobby and Chrissie. They would probably go through life not knowing about geography or history or how to make a graph. They'd never know life outside The Farm. A picture of Mimi writing in her journal formed in Nell's mind. Students in Emma's class would never know the joy of a new green notebook with clean lined paper inside.

All multiplication. Nell hadn't missed anything. She did the problems quickly, then searched through Emma's pile of books for something to read.

"I have more of the Wilder series you like so much," Emma said.

"Families aren't like that. Can't I cook in the kitchen? I know how to make bread and pies, and I even know how to pasteurize milk. I could get up early and make the coffee so the kitchen ladies could sleep later."

Emma put a book in front of Nell. "Children aren't allowed in the kitchen. It's much too dangerous, and you'd only get in the way. Try this book. It's about a girl and her grandfather who live in the Alps."

Concentrating was hard with Bobby multiplying out loud and the Middles learning their tables. At least the book wasn't about Ma and Pa and their good little girls. Also, Heidi had no mother or father, and Nell knew how that felt.

The clatter in the kitchen pulled her attention from the book, back to Ilse's saying something about those wasted years. For twelve years her mother had been planting herbs and talking with people who only spoke about life on The Farm. After glimpsing her mother's life in the yearbook, Nell wondered how Ilse had stayed so long on The Farm, where she had no chance to play her flute or work on a magazine or read more books. Nell looked around her. The children plodded through their daily math examples, without any of the excitement of Mrs. Cavendish's pupils. Nell wondered if she wanted to be a child in this big family anymore. After all, she knew how to cook and how to multiply, and there were so many other things she needed to learn. And she wouldn't learn them here.

19

Lights flicked on around the dining hall long before dinnertime. Nell curled in a soft chair with *Heidi*, feeling like she was on vacation. Abigail was taken care of, someone else was cooking dinner, and the animals were fed and milked, all without Nell's help. She raced through the book, expecting to be called to duty at any minute.

At the slam of the door, *Heidi* slipped from Nell's hands and skidded across the floor, coming to rest at Tip's feet. He scooped Nell out of the chair. "I've been frantic. The house was empty, the furnace off, and the pipes frozen. When I found your note I called up here and reached Alice, who said you girls were fine. I walked back to town to pick up the truck. How did you get here if the truck was behind the IGA?"

Tip smelled like fresh, cold air, and Nell clung fiercely to him. "I was afraid you'd frozen in Boston," she whispered. She didn't add her worst fear, the one that had sneaked into her early-morning terror. Tip did love her, she felt certain of that.

"The lines were down and I couldn't call out. I assumed you were all right." He sat in the chair and held her on his lap. "Abigail okay?"

"She has a cold, but she's with the Wee Ones, so I guess she's all right." Tip's brace cut into her legs and she shifted slightly. "The storm was over days ago."

"We had to put off a meeting until people could get into the city. Only ambulances and police cars were allowed through for two days. As soon as the meeting was over I got on the first bus that left town. I called from the drug store, and when no one answered, I walked to the house." He lifted Nell down and struggled to his feet. "I still don't understand about the truck. How did you get here? Is Ilse outside?"

Nell thought back to the note she had written. She had said, *We're at The Farm*. Tip didn't know the "we" meant just herself and Abigail.

People began to come into the dining hall. Nell caught sight of Emma and Jim, and remembered that *Heidi* was still lying on the floor. She darted forward to pick it up as Tip asked again, "Where's your mother?"

Nell stalled. The Moores steered her to a table and motioned for Tip to join them.

"I don't understand," Tip said. "Ilse was taking care of the girls when I left. She could have called someone to fix the furnace. Why did she bring the children here?"

"She didn't," Emma said. "We did. Nell was in trouble

and she called us. We haven't questioned her. I knew sooner or later the story would come out."

Tip held his head in his hands in a way that frightened Nell. She tried to make him feel better. "Mom left, Dad. The day after you did. She went to New York. She knew you'd be right back, so she didn't worry about us. And she left us plenty of food and a load of hay."

He hit his forehead with the palm of his hand. "Forgot all about Rose. Didn't even check to see if she had been milked." Tip was so upset, even Emma seemed to feel sorry for him.

"I think we'd better get back to the beginning and get this story straight. Why don't you tell it from the beginning, Nell."

Nell clutched *Heidi* as she told of Tip's leaving, and of Ilse's letter in the mail. "She drove in to catch the bus the next day, Dad. She just couldn't wait." Nell told them about the storm, Rose's restlessness, and finally of finding Rose dead.

"That was the worst. Worse than having the furnace go off and the water freeze up. Every time I looked at Abigail I thought of finding her dead like Rose. I wasn't sure I could save her. I didn't want to call anyone in town and let them know we were alone, and you and Mom didn't leave me phone numbers, so I called Miz Moore, and here we are."

No one looked at Nell. Jim Moore examined his fingernails, Emma stared at the fireplace, and Tip still had his hands over his eyes.

"All she would say was that it was a mix-up," Jim said. "Some mix-up. Those kids could have frozen to death."

"Like Rose." Nell hit the table with tight fists. Rose had been in her care and Rose was dead. In the early morning, she had blamed herself for not taking better care of Rose, but now she felt anger as she began to think that Rose's death had not been all her fault. She was not the only one responsible for Rose and Abigail. Tip and Ilse were, too.

Now that Nell was angry, Tip began to calm down. "I'm here, now, and everything's going to be all right. Gather your things and Abigail's, and we'll go home."

"Not at dinnertime, you won't," Emma said. "Those children haven't caught up on their sleep yet. Also, there's the matter of a cold house and no running water."

Tip agreed to stay the night in the old hayloft over the end of the dining hall, which The Farm had turned into a guest room. At dinner, the Willows sat with the Moores, and over Abigail's protests, Tip fed the baby every mouthful.

"Your mother went to New York. Do you remember any name on that letter?" he asked Nell.

Nell could not. "I think she took the letter with her."

Tip called the house in Blue Harbor on the chance that Ilse might be home and wondering where everyone was, but there was no answer. He paced the dining hall and never noticed when Nell and Abigail went back to the Moores' cabin.

A night's rest simmered Tip down, though his fingers drummed restlessly on the breakfast table. "Let's go home, Nell. Your mother's not back yet, but we'll be all right. I can order a tank of oil from here. I'll call a plumber. By the time we get home, everything will be fixed."

Nell squirmed. Her bedroom under the eaves was so much nicer than the cot in the Moores' cabin. Jack waited at Mimi's house. Her school desk sat smack against Mimi's desk, with all her books ready to be read. The tangy air of Maine called to her, but even with all the good things that she missed, she was afraid to go back. She had been responsible for almost everything when they lived in Maine, and had not done such a good job. Maybe it would be better to stay on The Farm and be just another young person with no responsibilities. Nell took a long time, thinking of the good and bad, for Abigail as well as herself.

Tip got up and stomped impatiently around the table, stopping only when Nell whispered a shaky, "No." His face reddened.

"I want to go back with you, Dad." She touched his hand. "I know you love us. I probably could do better this time, work harder and take care of things. But Abigail needs more. You and Ilse need to finish your writing, and you'll close yourselves in the front room again. Nothing will change. Abigail will be happier here with the Wee Ones, and I should stay and help her learn to talk and play."

Tip steamed up, ignoring her argument. "I'll just carry you to the car."

The look on his face frightened Nell. She had never gone against him and wasn't sure what he'd do.

Emma broke into the conflict before she could find out. "Tip, I want to know why you left the children in the first place."

"Boston called. I sent them part of my book, and they wanted to talk about it. The storm slowed the meeting, but the editors said they were interested. I've got to go back home and start working again."

"You could work here until your book is done," Nell said. "Maybe we could get our cabin back until you finished. Then, when you have more time for things, we could go back to Maine."

Tip slammed the table. "It's the same old story. That book may make some money, and I don't want to give it to The Farm. First the army took care of me, and then The Farm did. Now *I* want to take care of me and my family."

"But you're not taking care of them, don't you see?" Emma said. "The children need more care than you're giving them."

The air left Tip in a long, slow hiss. He seemed to grow smaller.

"I'm fine," Nell said stoutly. "It's just Abigail who needs care." She looked over to the table where the Big Ones sat, ready to do the day's multiplication. If they lived on The Farm the rest of their lives, they might never use math.

Hi Grady joined them. "Heard about your cow, Willow. She was a pretty one. We should have insisted on helping you with the shed last fall."

Tip stiffened, the way he had at the barbecue.

"Why was it all right to work together here, and not all right at Blue Harbor, Dad?"

Emma hugged Nell. "Oh, my, yes. She is right. We should have helped you at the start, but I think we were too angry at you for leaving. The men could have helped you with the buildings, and I should have seen to it the children were cared for. What we need to do is find care for Abigail."

"Maybe Dad could work at the shrimp-processing plant," Nell said. "Mimi's father works there." She told them about all the children and the dogs. "We could live like they do, I know we could," she said excitedly. "Tip would go to work like other fathers, and Ilse could stay home and take care of Abigail. They could write later, when Abigail goes to school."

"Not all families are alike, Nell," Emma said. "Somehow I can't see Tip working in a factory, or Ilse baking bread."

Nell slipped off the bench and walked over to sit next to Bobby. Nothing was going to get settled with Tip so stubborn. She might as well buckle down and learn something. One of the kitchen women was filling in for Emma as teacher, and she had them write letters on the rough paper that was handed out, one sheet at a time.

Dear Mimi, . . . Nell began.

20

The dark sky turned the snow to gray, the trees to black ink drawings, and the windows inside the dining hall to mirrors. No one talked, not even the Wee Ones. A storm threatened The Farm, silencing even the chain saw.

A thick wool cap confined Tip's black curls. Abigail reached for his hair, putting chubby fingers inside the cap, singing "Twinkle" as she did so.

Nell was as uncertain as the storm. Tip was going to leave without her. She wished she had a book to help her understand, but there was no book that told of a mother gone and a father leaving.

"Can't you wait until the storm passes?" Nell asked.

"Ilse may be back without any heat or water. I'll take the long way around since the mountain pass is closed. Besides, Hi and Jim will be with me. We can watch out for each other. The sooner I get this project started, the sooner you girls can come home.

"Be good," Tip whispered to Abigail, as if she had been a terrible child and needed a warning. "Be good," he said again to Nell. She would have liked it better if he'd told her to clean the chicken coop or bake a loaf of bread. Be good? Life wasn't about being good or bad. It was about doing or not doing, and suddenly she had nothing to do.

"As soon as things are back together again, I'll come and get you," he whispered fiercely. He pulled one of Nell's dark curls so it bounced back, a spring released.

"I could make your dinner and mind Abigail," she said as forlornly as a lamb who had lost its mama.

"This time it will be different. Hi and Jim are going with me to warm the house and fix the pipes. They're even going to help me make a schedule like the one hanging on the wall here to tell me what I have to do. When everything's ready, I'll come back and get you both."

Nell wished she hadn't wanted to come back here. She must have wanted too hard. The Farm wasn't home. It was like kindergarten, and she was in the fifth grade.

Emma lifted Abigail from Tip's arms. "Go along with you," she said, swatting the baby on the bottom. Abigail ran in her stomach-out, bowlegged way over to the Wee Ones in the pillowed corner.

Nell found herself enveloped in Tip's arms, felt the scratchiness of his cheek, the softness of his voice against her ear. "I'll let the school know you'll be back soon. A few weeks and we'll be back to normal. No. Better than normal."

She kissed his bristly cheek, then stood sturdily on

two feet. "Won't you tell Emma I can work in the kitchen?"

"They have their rules. Be a little girl for a few weeks."

After the men left, Nell took her coat and went outside. A light drizzle had started, just enough to turn the snow on the road to slush, but not enough to melt the snowbanks at the side of the road.

After almost a year of having something to do every minute, she felt empty. Invisible. Fog rose in clouds from the snowbanks, shrouding the barn, the tractor shed, and the building where the wool was washed and carded in its thick blanket. She was lost in an unreal world of unfamiliar shapes.

Through the dusty, straw-flaked window of the sheep barn Nell saw the round bodies of the sheep. There were no lambs, only fat, slow-moving animals, their tangled wool dirtied by straw and mud. She had warned those leaping babies not to grow up, but they had, anyway.

Nell turned away. She had grown up, too. Like Tip and Ilse, she was lost between two worlds.

The dull days passed slowly. Schoolwork was uninteresting, and Nell was too restless to read. Tip and Ilse were always on her mind. She talked to them in her head, urging Tip to hurry back, and Ilse to come home. The one-sided conversation droned on with no answer.

Hi and Jim returned from Maine. Nell heard Jim talking to Emma in their bedroom. "We got a lot done. The ground was too frozen to bury you-know-what, so we hired a man with a truck to pick it up. Had to replace the pipes in the bathroom, but the rest of the plumbing was all right. Oil burner's humming. We worked out a schedule with Tip."

His voice dropped. Nell raised her ear from the pillow, straining to hear. "He got in touch with her. Didn't say much. She did most of the talking. She's not home, though."

That meant Ilse was all right. Surely she had to come home. All she had taken was that one little suitcase. What would life in the farmhouse be like if she never came home? Tip would be the only one working in the front room, and Abigail would have no mother. Nell wouldn't, either.

February brought birthday time. Nell thought back to last year. Ilse had given her a potpourri of herbs and rose leaves, and Tip had made a wooden barrette to hold back her dark curls. This year, with no family except Abigail, Nell expected nothing.

"Your father called," Emma said, quivering with delight. "He's coming for your birthday dinner with a surprise. He told us to be your parents and get you what you want most."

Nell escaped to the frozen stream that had been their wading place in the summer. In spots the ice was so clear she could see water trickling along the rocks on the bottom. Almost a year ago she, Bobby, and Chrissie had played here in the afternoons. Since she'd been back, she'd hardly ever visited the stream, as if it was part of a childhood that was over.

Bobby came sliding down the bank, his feet deserting him as he reached Nell. "What ya doing?" he asked from his sitting position.

"Just thinking what I'd like for my birthday."

He stood and wiped snow and ice from his pants. "You know the things they sell on the outside. And your father's got money. If I were you, I wouldn't know what to ask for. Did you ever go in a store?"

"Sure. I bought a candy necklace, all different colors. You could wear them and eat them at the same time. And I bought books. And a white horse on wheels for Abigail."

"Sassafras," Bobby said. It was his mother's favorite swear word. "Can boys wear those necklaces?"

"I guess so." Since candy interested Bobby more than books or a wooden horse, she began to list the penny candies for sale in the store with the slanting floors.

"So, what do you want for your birthday?"

She took a slide on the ice. "My mother home. But your parents can't bring Ilse back. And Jack, but I'll pick him up when I get home." She thought. "Maybe another Rose."

"A rose? In February?"

Nell laughed. "A cow, scherzo. A red cow."

Bobby licked his lips as if tasting the penny candy. "Don't know if Ma will get you a cow. Better think some more."

On her birthday, Nell wandered around the dining hall long before dinnertime. Tip could show up at any minute.

Then he was there, clumping across the floor, arms waving, and hair flying. He was not carrying anything. Oh no, not Christmas all over again, she thought.

After the hugs and handshakes, the Willows and the

Moores settled on the benches at the Moores' table. Birthday dinners were special, shared by everyone. Nell was bursting with questions but waited patiently while Tip happily plowed through the roast chicken and stuffing. He probably had eaten dry cereal and peanut butter without Nell there to cook for him.

The tables were cleared, and cakes brought out, one for each table, though Nell's was the only one with candles. She blew them out quickly.

"And now for my presents," Tip said. He leaned back as if pleased with himself. "Thought I'd forgotten, didn't you?"

Nell shook her head in a solemn, silent lie.

"The first present is that tomorrow I'm taking you and Abigail home."

It was not a bought present, but it was a surprise. By her own rules, the surprise made it a present. It was what she had wished for. She decided that when they got home, she would teach Tip that sometime she would like to get something in a box and tied with a ribbon. But for now, it was enough just to get home.

"Are you sure things have changed?" Nell asked Tip. She desperately wanted to go back to Maine, but not if life would be the way it had been.

"Ask Hi and Jim, and Emma, too. They did most of the planning, and they know what you and Abigail need. Believe me, things will be different. I'll tell you all about it on the way home."

Nell looked around the table, seeing the smiles and nods from Emma and Jim.

"You'll be fine," Emma assured her.

"The second present is one I couldn't wrap, either. Jim, Hi, and I made that shed over into the sweetest, tightest little building in the whole of Maine. Not"—he held up a hand in warning—"not for another cow. A cow just doesn't fit into my new schedule. It's for a playhouse for you and your friends."

This was a new idea. She had rarely ever played in Maine, and she wasn't sure she wanted to. Also, going into Rose's shed was not what she wanted most to do. Maybe, when you reached twelve, you didn't play anymore. Nell thought of Mimi. Between the two of them they might find *something* they could do with the shed. Mimi could have fun wherever she was.

"I think the present we got Nell would like the shed better than her friends would." Emma handed Nell a real birthday card. Inside was a carefully printed promise: *One lamb to be delivered as soon as it can travel.*

21

Abigail held her legs stiff and cried, "No, no," when Tip tried to put her in the car seat. A fierce wind had chapped her cheeks in the short walk from the Moores' cabin, and fury reddened them more. Nell was certain another tantrum was on the way, and she was glad Abigail was angry at Tip for a change. Tip ignored Abigail, just held her firmly and maneuvered each rigid leg into the seat. Nell climbed into the truck, grateful to be inside, even though it meant that Ilse was not with them.

"The road through the mountains is still closed," Tip said. "The long way around will add an extra hour or two." He gave Abigail a worried look as if he feared she might cry the entire way home. But the motion of the truck acted like a magic potion, closing her eyes and lulling her to sleep.

Nell tucked a blanket around her sister. "She had a good time with the Wee Ones, Dad. She trotted over there after breakfast, and every time I looked over, she was smiling. I think she needs to see other kids."

Tip nodded as he avoided some snow drifting across the road. "Emma thought so, too. That's why I've arranged for her to stay with the Tompkinses during the day. There are enough children in that house to keep her happy."

Nell's heart flip-flopped. "How great. Mrs. Tompkins is the best."

"You're to go there after school. I'll pick both of you up about four."

Nell reached across the sleeping Abigail to squeeze her father's hand. Imagine being told she had to walk home with Mimi every afternoon!

The road dipped into the shadow of a mountain where patches of ice glistened treacherously. Tip slowed down.

"Where's Mom?" Nell asked.

Tip's good hand gripped the steering wheel. "She's staying with a college friend in New York for a while."

"I saw her yearbook. I looked in yours, too. You and Mom are so different."

"We met in Boston. I was just out of the hospital. I could barely talk and had a hard time walking. Everything was hard for me—I even had to learn how to use my left hand for eating and dressing myself. I was waiting in line to go into a movie, and your mother was next in line. We started talking. Later we went to a coffee house and talked half the night."

When they crossed the Maine border, Tip was still talking. Nell barely breathed, afraid that any little noise might silence him. Nothing did, though, not even a stop for lunch at a diner, or another stop for gas.

"Ilse was tall, bright, and beautiful. Her father died when she was eight." Nell gasped, thinking of how much she had missed Tip the few days he had been gone. Her mother had had a whole lifetime of missing her father.

"When we met, she was about to graduate from college, and her mother wanted her to come home. Ilse needed to get away from her mother, who had brought her up to be a perfect student. I needed to get away from mine, who thought I couldn't do anything on my own. We turned to each other."

Nell had never heard how they had met, but it was not hard to picture them as two lost children. "And The Farm?" she asked to keep Tip talking.

"I met Hi and Joe at a veterans' meeting. Hi's family owned the land in Vermont. The three of us came up with the idea of The Farm."

"And me and Abigail?"

"Ilse and I got married the day we opened the dining hall. We both wanted children very much."

Tip settled into his driving. Nell closed her eyes and saw a tall girl in a plaid skirt standing outside a movie house beside a good-looking man with dark, curly hair. The most-likely-to-succeed and the ex-soldier broken by the war. Then she fell into a dreamless sleep.

Nell unlocked the front door and stepped into the warm hall. Stairs to the right, kitchen straight ahead, the front room to her left. Home.

"Ma, ma," Abigail said.

"No Mama. Say Daddy," Tip said matter-of-factly. He put her on her feet and went out for their trash bags full of clean clothes. What were they going to do about clothes and shopping and a garden in the summer? Tip's words, "No Mama," stabbed Nell. How could there be a house without a Mama?

The white horse waited in the kitchen. "Orsey, orsey," Abigail said. "Orsey wants cookie." She smiled up at Nell.

Abigail remembered things, Nell realized. "I'll make some cookies later," she promised.

The pots that had held water were put away and the cage of chairs was gone. A bowl of green apples in the center of the table seemed to be waiting to be made into pie.

Nell wandered the rooms, feeling the ghost of Ilse in each of them. Ilse typing in the front room, Ilse at the kitchen table, Ilse sleeping late the morning after the barbecue. There were no ghosts in Nell's room, just her oak leaf and her books, and her journal now tucked in a drawer. Nell went back downstairs.

Tip talked after dinner, a dinner he made. "It's all coming together," he said. "The trouble was in the beginning when we left The Farm in such a hurry. We had no time to sit down and plan what we wanted and what we needed to do. Hi and Jim helped me plan."

"Do you think Mom will come back?"

His dark eyes clouded. "Right now she feels her poetry is the most important thing. All those years on The Farm, she put her own dreams aside. I think both of us are stronger now. We can live on the outside. Once she's finished what she has to do, maybe she'll come back. She needs more time."

"Mothers don't leave children. Ma Ingalls wouldn't. Neither would Daniel's mother, or Mimi's."

"Those friends of yours are very special. When I checked in at school, Mr. Quimby told me about them. Everyone's waiting for you to come back to school. And Jack is ready to come here."

Nell considered this. "I was never sure if you heard me when I told you about Jack."

"I don't think I did. But when I talked to Mrs. Tompkins about taking care of you girls, she asked me when we were going to pick up your dog. I'll pick up the three of you at four tomorrow afternoon."

"I don't know if I'm ready to go back to school, Dad. And what am I supposed to do now that things have changed?"

Tip reached over and held her hand firmly. "Emma and I talked about that. I'm to drop the laundry off when I take Abigail to the Tompkinses' house. I guess you'll still be the main cook, but I'm Abigail's father, and I intend to work harder at that. You taught her to sing, I can teach her to talk. You'll be a fifth-grader who helps her father while your mother is away."

There was too much to think about. Nell was tired down to her bones. "When you take Abigail in the morning, could you drop me off at the wharf? I'd like to walk across the bridge with Daniel."

A cold, blue day without a touch of wind. More than one storm seemed to be over, Nell thought. The sea beyond the harbor stretched flat and motionless to the horizon. Daniel, in his blue jacket, met her at the edge of the wharf, and the two of them waved to Daniel's mother sitting at the window.

"I missed you," Daniel said. "It was lonely, walking to school alone."

He looked older, as if those hours waiting for his father to come back from sea had made him grow up.

"I missed you, too," Nell confessed. "It's so wonderful to be in the real world again. I just don't know if I'm ready." She wondered if Bobby would ever grow up or if he would go through life wishing for penny candy. She needed to shake the mixed-up feelings of the past weeks, and fill her lungs with the clean Maine air she'd longed for, for so long. "Race you!" she cried.

Nell and Daniel raced across the bridge, and once around the school yard, Mimi joining in as they reached the school.

"Are there any streams near your house?" Nell asked. "I miss playing by a stream."

"Sure thing," Mimi said. "There's one cutting through the back of our property. Kind of frozen right now, though. But we can take Jack and slide around this afternoon."

"I'd like to come, too. That is, if you don't mind," Daniel said. "Maybe we can dam up a pond so we can skate next winter."

By the time the bell rang, Nell felt more like a fifth-grader than she'd felt in a long time.

The walls inside Blue Harbor Elementary School had red hearts pasted on them. Nell had forgotten the day and for a minute thought they were welcome-home signs. The fifth grade classroom was decorated, too, and folders full of valentines were taped to the desks. Nell's folder bulged, which meant Mimi had told the class she was coming home.

Mrs. Cavendish hurried toward her, a welcoming smile on her face, and a copy of the class newspaper in her hand. The dittoed papers were stapled together, and the front page had a poem by Nell Willow. It was the one she'd worked on so long ago, and she had sent it in that letter to Mimi. Nell had never seen her name in print before. So many "L"s.

She sat down, cheeks burning, and held the paper up to hide her face as she read.

Baby's white horse gallops
From kitchen to the hall.
Mom and Dad spin miles of words
Through winter, spring, and fall.
I walk from stove to sink
And go nowhere at all.

"How did that poem get in there?" she whispered to Mimi.

"You sent it in your letter, and I gave it to Mrs. Cavendish."

"Thanks a lot," Nell said, not sure if she meant it or not. She made a face, and Mimi crossed her eyes. Just like the old days.

Nell took the folded green notebook out of her pocket. She had not written in it since that day she and Abigail waited for Emma. It was time, now, to write.

This afternoon I walk with Mimi to her house. Abigail and Jack are there. Daniel may come over, too. Dad will pick us up and drive us home.

She looked up. Daniel rummaged in his desk for his math book, his hair standing like the grasses in the snow. Mimi rearranged her desk, keeping it neat. At home the little ones mixed up her things.

Mrs. Cavendish began a lesson in fractions, then stopped to walk to Nell's desk. "Mimi can help you with fractions later," she whispered. "This morning you are to fill up your notebook. Put your past where it belongs."

Nell bent over her notebook again. *Ilse did not come home.* Her knuckles stiffened as she wrote the words. *I miss her. Abigail needs her. But she needs her poetry. It feels good to see a poem in print. I know.*

Mrs. Cavendish drew circles on the board to explain fractions that were equal to one whole. The lesson fascinated Nell. If the circle was cut into four pieces and all four pieces were shaded, then the four parts equalled one whole. 4/4 = 1. If Tip, Ilse, Abigail, and Nell were four in a family, then all four of them equalled one whole family. But if the circle was divided into three parts and there were only Tip, Abigail, and Nell, then the three of them would equal one family. 3/3 = 1.

Soon a lamb will come to live in the shed. It won't stay frisky forever, but I will love it even when it grows up. It will live in the shed that Tip fixed. I will name it Swanli, like Grandfather's goat in Heidi. *Tip will take care of us. He will write his book about the war. We will take care of each other. I think we'll be all right, even if Ilse does not come home.* Her eyes stung as she wrote the last words. Her eyes were just tired from the first day of being in the outside world, she decided.

The recess bell rang. Nell didn't mind missing fractions, but there was no way she was going to miss recess. She had just one more line to add. Skipping a blue line in the notebook, she printed in capital letters,

TODAY I TAKE JACK HOME!!!